He
Cowboy's Wedding Fiasco

A billionaire in need of a temporary wife, a vineyard owner in need of an investor fast, a wedding proposal that could save them both, but can they survive the three-month timeline?

To save his Texas vineyard, billionaire Todd McCoy has to marry within three months and stay married for three months or he loses it all; the vineyard, the wine and the grape jelly McCoy Stonewall Vineyards is famous for. Not happy with his granddaddy but not willing to lose everything he's worked so hard for, Todd's planning on answering the challenge…

Ginny Rossi loves the small vineyard and the boutique wine business she and her parents have built. Then her parents decide to retire and sell the vineyard. She has less than four months to find the money to buy them out before they sell her out. She needs a miracle. The last thing she expects is her best friend's new brother-in-law, who grates on her every nerve, to show up with a proposal she can't refuse…one that will be beneficial to both of them.

If they can survive three months, they can both walk away with what they love most in all their world, their vineyards. *If* they can survive.

Among the grapes and vines will they fall in love?

HER BILLIONAIRE COWBOY'S WEDDING FIASCO

McCoy Billionaire Brothers, Book Two

HOPE MOORE

Her Billionaire Cowboy's Wedding Fiasco

Copyright © 2019 Hope Moore

CHAPTER ONE

"What a *fiasco*. I knew this was going to happen." Todd McCoy stared at Cal Emerson, his grandfather's lawyer. Granddaddy had obviously lost his mind right before he'd passed away a little over six months ago. Before he'd left them, he'd redone his will to make all his grandsons suffer by forcing them to get married, at least he was assuming all of them would. Since first up was Wade, and he'd married, now Cal was able to reveal Todd's fate which was similar to Wade's—but Morgan's actual requirements wouldn't be revealed until he either accomplished his challenge or lost everything. And that was the kicker—why had Granddaddy made his demands a do it or else lose it all, everything they had worked so hard for and loved? Wade had been first and ended up, as crazy as it was, happily married to Allie, whom he'd married in order to save the ranch he'd helped build.

Now, it was Todd finding out his fate.

He gripped the edge of the chair he sat in. He'd watched the last three months while Wade had jumped through hoops to save the ranch and now Wade sat beside him, as happy as a clam, still married and deeply in love.

But even so, Todd was *not* going to be a puppet on a string.

He loved his grandfather but this was going too far. J.D. McCoy had been used to getting his way. He'd brought his grandsons up to like hard work and to be proud of what they were building. Todd loved producing the best grape jelly the world had ever tasted, and he truly believed that McCoy Stonewall Jelly was the best, and he had helped build the multibillion dollar enterprise they all had dedicated their lives to. Todd was also proud of the wine they were producing but his pride and joy was the jelly production. And his granddaddy knew this.

He knew it, and he'd given Todd full rein to take the jelly company to new heights, and Todd had run with it in the years that he'd had complete control of that division of McCoy Enterprises. And now, from the grave, his grandfather was going to take his passion away from him.

Just like that.

The thought of losing the jelly farm and the winery twisted him into knots.

"I'm going to have to jump through the same hoops that Wade did if I want to save the vineyards, save the jelly brand and the wine? There is no other way?" He knew there wasn't, knew his granddaddy had lost his ever-lovin' mind to do this to him, and yet he asked anyway. He was desperate.

Mr. Emerson didn't even bother saying yes; he just nodded. And smiled.

"Don't give me that, Cal. There's got to be more

in that will than just a nod from you." Unable to continue sitting, Todd stood and strode to the window, where he grabbed the frame and stared out across the ranch that they all loved so much. At least they didn't have to worry about losing it any longer. Wade had saved it.

Now it was his turn—*His turn.*

"Todd, it's the same as it was with Wade, if you want to save your vineyards, to be clear, McCoy Stonewall Jelly and Wine Division and keep it in the control of you and your brothers, then you have three months to find a wife, then three months to stay married. Because it worked out for Wade, he kept the stipulations the same."

"Does that mean if it hadn't worked out for me, then Todd's stipulations would have been different?" Wade beat Todd to the question. And from the corner where Morgan stood, stiff and unmoving, a grunt of disgust sounded.

They watched as Cal steepled his fingers then nodded slowly.

"That does it," Morgan growled. "He has

contingency plans?"

Another nod.

That darn nod was growing old. Todd hung his head. "Even from the grave, he's thought of everything. Sounds just like him."

"Yes, he did. Now, I'm not allowed to elaborate more. But I need to again reassure you boys that your granddaddy was not crazy, not losing his senses, and not being vengeful. He wanted heirs; none of you boys seemed in a hurry to get married and he had grown weary of waiting. So even though he knew that in the end you might still never marry even after the stipulations he laid out, he wanted to…encourage you to try."

"You mean force us."

Cal's lips twitched. "As you can see, Wade thought that J.D. was playing a little poker with y'all and that he was bluffing, but I can assure you he wasn't. I have my orders, so that's the deal. When you walk out that door, the clock starts ticking."

Morgan growled, "This is ridiculous. Todd has built that business into what it is. Yes, it had a name and reputation when we were growing up, but until Todd took over ten years ago at eighteen and put his marketing genius behind it and tweaked those grapes into tasting like they do today, there was no comparison. And now, he stands to lose that? I don't agree with any of this."

Everything Morgan said was true and Todd felt a sense of pride that his older brother acknowledged that. Yeah, it made him proud. But he also knew Morgan could feel the clock ticking and his time was coming. And Morgan had built McCoy Stonewall Hotel and Resort Division into what it was today: a powerhouse that could compete on a global market. Granddaddy was heartless. That was all there was to this.

But if there was one thing Todd knew, it was that when the chips were down, he was not the kind of man who would be counted out. He would not let himself be that man. And his granddaddy knew it.

So, what now? "Thanks, Morgan, and I agree with you. Granddaddy knows that I'm a part of that land, that my roots are in that dirt. Just like Wade's are in this ranch. And while your roots are in the land, too, you just have a different calling in the hospitality industry. We love what we do; it's in our blood. Just like it was in Granddaddy's. But as much as I hate to say it, I can see his point. What man who's built all this, watched us flourish in it, wouldn't want great-grandkids? We just happened not to be in any hurry and, we did, or do, give off the vibe that we're not going to get married. I know I'm not commitment material. I'm not ready." He looked at Wade. "That's how you felt, too, wasn't it?

"In many ways." Wade smiled. "And as mad as I was, it all worked out and I found the best woman in the world. I'm glad I took the challenge. But just because it worked out for me doesn't mean it will for you. But I'm rooting for you. And that's what Granddaddy wanted, I think—for us to just take a shot at it."

"But I don't want to take a shot at it."

"Exactly," Morgan agreed with Todd.

Todd raked his hand through his hair, resigned to the idea. No, he wasn't happy—he wasn't happy at all—but he was not going to lose everything he had worked so hard for. "As much as I despise this idea, I know when I'm going to have to give in and go for it. But mark my words: it's going to take a miracle and I mean a pure miracle for me to even proposition some unsuspecting female to even do this. I don't like my chain being yanked and if and when I do get married for real, I'm going to pick her not because of some scheme Granddaddy concocted to force me."

Turning without saying another word, he strode out the door and into the sunshine. His gut churned and his temper boiled. He needed a miracle.

Ginny Rossi stared at her parents in total and complete disbelief. *What?* "You are *not,* cannot be selling this winery. Where is this thought even coming from?"

Her parents had started the winery when she was a kid. She'd been brought up playing beneath the vines as a toddler and grown up with the business and then into the business. By the time she'd been an adolescent, it was her passion. It was her dream to build it into the best small label boutique Texas winery in the country and she was well on her way. But now—this? "What are y'all thinking?" She repeated what she had said in her mind out loud, glaring at them.

"Now calm down, sunshine." Her daddy raked a hand down his face, meeting her gaze with one stern look of his own. "We didn't come to this conclusion without a lot of thought."

"You're telling me you two have been scheming behind my back." She had his grit and mettle, that was for sure, but he had raised her to speak her mind and she wasn't backing down now just because he was speaking his. She wanted to hear why they were tearing her world from beneath her.

"Your mom and I want to retire, and yes, we're thinking about you, too. This offer came out of the blue. It surprised us and got us to thinking. The offer is generous and far exceeds any amount that we could ever imagine. It will set us up for our retirement and we won't have to worry about if we're going to make our money back this year with the crop and cases of wine. And we can travel instead of being tied to the harvest and the production schedules. But it's not just about us—this money will set you up, too. You won't ever have to worry about anything. We'll invest that money and you'll be fine. We thought this would be a good time for you to have some freedom and figure out what you really want out of life. Maybe you can have time to find a husband and have a family. And if a winery ends up being what you want, you can start another winery."

Her mother looked at her with gentle eyes. "It wasn't as if you chose the winery. You were just born into it. Have you ever thought there might be some other passion out there you'd like to pursue? This gives you that opportunity."

This was unbelievable. They just didn't get it. "No. I love this place. I feel blessed that I was born and raised here. You can't just tear it out from under me." She did see their point; she did. It would set them up for retirement—they wouldn't have to worry every year about whether this small winery was going to make it. But the thought of a big conglomerate taking over her winery…it hurt. They'd bring it in under their label and the *Rossi Rose of Tyler Winery* name would disappear. Their name, all her hard work would go away. As if it had never existed. She had worked so hard to get their brand recognition. It was her heart.

Her heart.

She had to think. Taking a deep breath, she fought for time. "Okay, wait. Just wait." She held her hands up as if that was supposed to help her think better. "What if…what if I come up with a way to get you the money that you need? I mean, I can maybe come up with the money that will buy you two out and set you up almost as well as this other option could. I can put together something that could replace your part of the option."

Her mother looked worried and her dad just shook his head. "Ginny, you know I believe in you but this is just too much. I'm going to sell. You don't need to take it into debt and have that hanging over your head. You could lose it all. And you'll only work harder and not find out that there is more in life out there."

"I don't *want* to find out if there is more out there." Ginny shot out of the chair and paced. She

11

yanked her teal-toned cowboy hat off her head and slapped it against her leg as her mind whirled. "Dad, come on, give me six months. Don't do this to me."

He looked conflicted. "I can't. The deal closes in four months."

"Then give me that time at least. Dad, you've got to give me a shot at keeping my dream alive."

Her dad looked as though he were about ready to have a fit. He stared out the window, both hands on his jean-clad hips; his shoulders were stiff. His body language was not looking good. She would beg if she had to. Her mind was reeling. *What could she do?*

She pinned him with eyes full of all the desperation that she was feeling. "Come on, Dad. It's not like you're going to lose out on anything. You've got to give me a shot."

He met her stare with one of...of...she gasped as she realized what she saw in her father's eyes. *He didn't believe in her.* He didn't think she would come up with the money. Or he didn't believe she could make a go of it if she were able to borrow enough to pay him.

The realization cut deep. More than anything else could.

She straightened and crossed her arms, her eyes probably glowing with her anger. Anger that hid the hurt because she refused to show how badly his lack of belief hurt. "You owe me a shot at this. I have worked my butt off for this winery. I should have some choice in something that affects my life. *My life*."

"Fine. You've got it. But when you bring me the deal, if I'm not satisfied completely, I go with this other offer. And you can't argue. Is it a deal?"

"*Deal*," she snapped without hesitation. "I'd better get to work." And with that, she spun and stormed out of the room, so mad she could spit nails. But she had no time to waste venting. She got into her Jeep and burned rubber as she drove toward the north corner of her winery, where she could sit and think in solitude. She had to come up with a plan.

It was going to take a miracle and every creative idea she could come up with to find the kind of money she was going to need to save her dreams.

CHAPTER TWO

As soon as Allie McCoy saw her best friend's name on the phone screen, she tapped the Accept button. "Ginny, I'm so glad you called—"

"They're selling the winery to a corporation," Ginny said, without pausing to say hello. "The corporation is going to destroy it. They're going to take our label off and join us in with a whole bunch of different wines, probably grocery store grade…it's going to be horrible. But I'm not going to let it happen. I'm not. I'm looking for a deal. I need to buy them out."

Allie, with mouth ajar, listened to the rapid-fire words of her best friend. Her tough-as-nails friend who had always been her backbone, her protector, her take-charge kick-butt friend who she loved with all her heart. And she was upset. Terribly upset. Rossi Rose of Tyler was Ginny's heartbeat. Her love. *What were her parents thinking?*

"Ginny, calm down. I hear you and can't believe this."

Ginny let out a long sigh. "Me either," she said with a tone that, for a small instant, sounded lost and vulnerable.

That was the thing: Allie had always been the sedate, vulnerable one. Ginny was the tough one who, even if she had a weak moment, no one ever knew it. Allie wasn't even supposed to have ever witnessed it but she had, though seldom. Allie knew her friend very rarely broke.

They were so opposite as friends that they made a complete circle when their list of differences were posed against each other. Ginny helped her be braver, and she helped Ginny loosen up on her usually aggressive stance.

Allie had never heard Ginny so upset.

"It's true. I have to come up with a deal or they're going to do it. I have four months before the deal closes to come up with the money, and somehow to convince my dad not to sell. But Allie, I understand why he's doing it. They work so hard and as wonderful as I believe our small label wine is, they have to worry all the time about whether we're going to have a bad crop or if this is going to be the year that does us in. They want to retire and this is an offer that is basically a once-in-a-lifetime kind of offer."

"That's amazing for them. But terrible as far as you go."

"Exactly. But I believe that if I had full control that maybe I could turn everything around and I don't need what they need. I just don't want this to happen. I've got to figure out a way to come up with this money." She gave a gruff laugh. "What I need is a miracle like you had. I need a billionaire to walk into my life and offer me the deal of a lifetime with an end date. Not really, but you know what I'm saying." She sighed. "I'll figure this out. I just needed someone to vent to and I knew you would understand."

And she was the only person Ginny would tell something so personal. Ginny held people at arm's length—heck, football field's length.

Allie stopped breathing, as her brain rolled over everything that had happened that morning. Wade had come in and found her on the patio outside their bedroom, writing. Working on her new novel. She was giving it everything she had and was so excited. He sat down on the lounger and draped an arm around her shoulders then told her that his granddaddy had given Todd the same stipulations as he'd had or they'd lose the vineyards and all businesses associated with it. Todd had to get married or he would lose the jelly business and the winery. Allie couldn't see Todd and Ginny together, but, desperate times called for desperate measures. *Should she mention this?*

This could be the solution to both of their problems. But the two of them didn't get along at all. Shoot, they could hurt each other. She was going to have to ask Wade about this. *Before* she mentioned it to Ginny.

"Ginny, whatever you do, don't do anything rash. You've got four months to figure this out and come up with a plan that works. You need an investor—that can't be too hard, can it? Your wine has been hanging in there with the best and it's making a profit, isn't it?"

"Yes, it is, and it's gaining recognition. I just think my dad is not giving it enough time."

"Okay, well, it just happened this morning, so just calm down and take a few deep breaths, you know. Take out your pad and pencil and write down your options. Do you want me to fly down there? We could meet up and maybe I could help?" "No, it's okay. I'll tell you what—if I need you, I'll holler. But you're right. I just need to calm down. I need to write things down and look at them and then I need to come up with a plan. You always know how to calm me down, to talk me off a cliff."

Allie chuckled. "And you always know how to push me off a cliff."

They laughed. It was so true.

As soon as Allie hung up the phone, she dialed

Wade's number.

"Hey, darlin'. Didn't I just see you?"

"Yes, you did. But something very interesting has just happened."

"Oh, really? More interesting than what I told you earlier about Todd having to find him a wife in three months? Deja vu all over again. Man, I'm hoping he finds a woman at least halfway as good as you. I don't think he can find one as good as you; don't think—I know he can't."

Her heart soared. She loved that man so much. Never in her wildest dreams had she thought a cowboy could walk into a truck stop and then the next day she'd be married to him, a cowboy billionaire. It was too crazy to believe and too unbelievable that in all the craziness, they had actually fallen in love.

"Well, actually, it kinda is. Ginny just called. And her parents are going to sell the winery to a corporation. For big bucks. So they can retire. And it's going to make Ginny lose everything she cares for, just like the way you felt when you were going to lose your ranch and just how Todd feels right now. The same thing is happening to Ginny. And she's not going to put up with it. She's got four months before the deal to come up with the money to stop her dad from selling. Wade, she needs a billionaire." She didn't say anything else; she didn't say what she was thinking because it was so hard to believe that one, it could be happening and two, the fireworks between those two were not good.

Wade got really quiet on the other end of the phone. "Allie, do you think?" Neither one of them said anything. "No...I can't even suggest what I'm thinking."

She chuckled. "I know, right? They would kill each other. They did not get along at all when Ginny came down a month ago. But..."

"Yeah, but they could help each other. The only problem with that is that Granddaddy really wanted to give us a shot at a real marriage. And I can't say that I believe that what happened between you and me would ever happen between Todd and Ginny. Man, that Ginny...I mean, I like her and all and I'm glad you have her as a friend. She was always looking out for you and all. But I have to say, I could not even imagine being married to her."

"Hey, don't be talking bad about my friend. But seriously, I understand what you're saying. She speaks her mind, she's very blunt, and yeah, she is kinda hard to get along with sometimes. But you know Todd—he's not in the best of moods either. I mean, he's nice to me but he's pretty grumpy."

"Yeah, darlin', you're right. And he really needs to get this done. The sooner he marries, the sooner he gets to have the final three months up. I'm going to mention this to him. That is what you wanted me to do, right?"

She groaned. "I really don't know, Wade. I didn't mention it at all to Ginny when she was telling me. I think all we can do is have you mention it to Todd, and I'll mention it to Ginny and then we're out of it. And they can figure out if they want to go through with this. They've got to decide if they think they can make it three months at least halfway getting along."

"You don't think she's going to bring Loretta out, do you?"

She laughed. "I'm not saying she's not going to

21

bring Loretta out because who knows." They both chuckled, knowing that Wade had almost met Loretta, the pink shotgun, face to face when Ginny had tried to make sure that he was going to do right by Allie.

"Well, all I can say is, if Todd does see a pathway to going through with this with Ginny, he's going to have to toe the line and not do anything that makes your buddy bring Loretta out."

"You know that's a lot of talk. She would never use Loretta on anything other than an intruder or attacker."

"I know, but she is intimidating."

"As she wants to be." She smiled. "And growing up, I loved having her beside me. No one messed with me."

"Good. That makes me happy. I kind of think she might be good for my brother."

Allie smiled. "You think so?"

"I do. You were very good for me, but Todd needs someone who can go toe-to-toe with him and your Ginny can. I hope it happens. It will be entertaining."

"Yes, it will."

CHAPTER THREE

Todd sat in his office, staring out at the grapes. He could still remember the day his grandfather had bought this piece of land. It had been a winery that had gone out of business and they'd gotten it for a song. And his granddaddy had done it because he could see the potential. Todd had been with him that day and also saw it. Todd liked ranching; he enjoyed riding his horse but he had always wanted to create something, build it from the ground up.

He had wanted to put his stamp on it and know that it hadn't been because of something his ancestors had done. And it hadn't been because of the oil that the McCoys were blessed with. No, this had taken him toiling and learning and researching and selling. And they were doing amazing. And now his grandfather was throwing this brick at him. He had to marry somebody. Now he just had to figure out who. In his mind, he went through the list of candidates, all women he had dated and stopped dating for one reason or another. None he'd wanted to marry.

He had friends from among some of them. But what friend did he have who would be willing to give up three months of her life for him? It was almost too much to ask. Miraculously, Wade had been able to do it. He wasn't sure he could. Grabbing his cell phone, he jumped to his feet and strode from his office, out the door and into the sunshine. He headed for the vines and waved at several of his men who were working with the vines. He strode down one of the vast number of rows of vines, leaving everything behind him as he kept walking down the path. His mind reeled and his thoughts filtered through everything and everyone he needed to consider. Who could he ask to do this temporary marriage? Because he wasn't kidding; he had no plans to stay married. His granddaddy wouldn't have that control over him. He didn't build this jelly business and wine business up, just to have his granddaddy yank it out from under him. No way, no how.

His phone rang. He tugged it out of his pocket and saw it was Wade. Probably calling to encourage him. His brother was so deliriously happy, he was practically spouting marshmallows, stars, and shamrocks.

He didn't even say hello. "If you've got advice, I'll take it. I'm so mad I could spit horseshoe tacks."

Wade chuckled. "And what's new about that? But I might be able to help you out. I have a very interesting development. One that seems to me to be, well, honestly, a miracle that could easily turn into a disaster."

Todd frowned. "What does that mean?"

"My sweet wife just told me that Ginny—you remember Ginny?"

"How could I forget the ill-tempered, bossy

cowgirl?"

The gorgeous bossy cowgirl.

Wade chuckled again. "That's what I thought you would say. Well, she's kind of in a bad situation and she needs to marry somebody with a bunch of zeros behind their name. It seems her parents are going to sell their winery out from underneath her for their retirement. And the only way she can stop it is if she can come up with the money to cover what they were getting from the corporation that's wanting to buy them out."

Todd stopped walking and muttered, "Holy smokes."

Ginny. The spitfire from central Texas. They'd gotten along like vinegar and oil but this was terrible for her.

"*Wow.*" He drew the word out in a long drawl as he let his thoughts whirl. "I see what you're saying. I certainly wouldn't call this an act of God. Ginny can't stand me, and I wasn't too fond of her either. She was here for five minutes and trying to tell me how to run my business. I couldn't imagine her here for three months. Can you imagine how she would be trying to get in my business?"

Wade laughed. "Maybe it wouldn't be that bad. But Allie is the one who thinks you two should join up and help each other out. She hasn't mentioned this to Ginny yet, but wanted to run it by me and you. Ginny is her best friend and she loves her. Ginny needs help, and you need help. But we don't want our relationships with either one of you to suffer, so don't do anything that you aren't comfortable with or think you can't do amicably."

Todd yanked his hat off his head, slapped it on his knee and glared at the dirt. He'd have to be crazy to consider this.

He'd have to be desperate.

You are desperate.

He groaned. "How long does she have?"

"The deal with her parents goes down in four months. It looks to me like the timing is right. The way I figure it, if you get married quick, you'd bypass the three-month period of finding a wife and go straight into the three months of staying married. You'd retain the vineyards and both jelly and wine business after that, free and clear."

"I would have to be desperate to bring her on to my property. But the fact is, I am desperate and I'm in a hurry. Why draw this out? Tell me again where she lives."

"You going down there?"

"Yeah. This doesn't seem like something you make a phone call about. Besides, I have a feeling that when she knows it's me, she'd hang up the phone. I'll take the jet."

There was a pause on the end of the line. At last, Wade let out a low whistle. "All right, I'll send you her address. And Todd…go easy. You do not want to get a tiger by the tail. You need this tiger in your corner for three months."

"Yeah, I know. Hopefully, she realizes she needs me as much as I need her…I can't even believe I just said that. But it's true. I do need her."

"Exactly."

Todd raked a hand through his hair and grimaced. "Here goes nothing."

The day after her parents had given her the news that they were selling out, Ginny walked out of the courthouse and into the bright sunshine. She'd been to see everyone she could think of and had gathered some help, but nowhere near enough. And in this situation, she knew it was all or nothing. She stared up at the cotton candy sky, as the bird's song rang from the trees. It was a beautiful day and she couldn't care less. She was drowning inside; it could've been a dark and stormy night for all she cared. She would not give up, though. It was a numbers game. She was going to get told no so many times; all she needed was a few yeses…right, a few yeses with a lot of zeros behind it. Truth be told, she didn't even know where to go to look for that kind of money.

She opened her eyes. Her brows dipped. *Allie had that kind of money now.* She hadn't even thought to ask Allie. But no; Allie had just married a billionaire. She wasn't going to jump in there and beg her best friend for money. No, she'd do this on her own. Thinking of Allie marrying a McCoy had Ginny's thoughts jumping instantly to that darn Todd McCoy. That man got under her skin. The handsome, smart-aleck cowboy had been interrupting her sleep lately. She stood there, thinking about the aggravating cowboy, and as if she conjured him up, suddenly she heard a slow drawl to her left. And she recognized it.

"Well, if it isn't Ginny Rossi. Fancy meeting you here on the doorstep of the courthouse."

Ginny slowly turned toward the sound of Todd McCoy's deep Texas drawl. Yup, there he was. He leaned against the concrete picnic table set under the big oak tree, his legs crossed. He wore shiny expensive boots, starched jeans, a brilliantly white starched button-up shirt with the sleeves rolled up to his elbows to expose muscled, tanned, *amazing* forearms and that set of hands that she had noticed when she had last seen him. Those arms were crossed over that hard chest and he had his head slightly cocked. His longish, sun-bronzed hair curled out from beneath the felt cowboy hat. And those steel-blue eyes that looked as though they were deep pools of icy water from the Guadalupe River lazily took her in as she stared at him.

The man let that gaze roll over her, making her very aware that she might not like him, but her inner woman, for some reason, reacted to him. She crossed her own arms and cocked her weight to one leg. She glared at the man with cool eyes. "Far as I know, cowboy, I'm in my territory. Question is, what are you doing here? Aren't you supposed to be back there at your little jelly bean farm?"

He chuckled. Those eyes held hers, unflinching. "It seems my little jelly farm doesn't grow beans. But it does a fine job with jelly. And grapes. And wine."

"Well, according to you. That still doesn't answer my question—what are you doing here? You're a long way away from home, I'd say about five hours."

"Actually, I've had a little dilemma come up. And I just heard a really oddball rumor that you also are in a little bit of a dilemma."

"What do you know?" Her eyes narrowed at the cowboy. *Had Allie told this jerk her business?* Okay, that wasn't fair and she knew it. She didn't like the dude but he was Allie's brother-in-law; she had probably told Wade what kind of problem she had, and he had probably mentioned it. She could not let that get her riled up.

"Well, actually, I've got a little bit of a problem, too, so we're even. The thing is, I think we could be mutually beneficial to each other. See, I have got to have me a wife before the end of three months. You've heard that line before, haven't you?"

"You have got to be kidding me. Your granddaddy did it to you too?"

Todd did not look happy as he nodded. "Yeah, you might say that. As he's so fond of saying, I'm the second domino to fall. Wade was lucky enough to be the first domino and I'm being facetious right there. And after me, it will be Morgan's turn to find out what his fate is. I'm sure Granddaddy did something equally terrible to him…might even be saving him for last to add a new devious twist to the plot. They butted heads all the time. He barely comes around even though he has a house on the ranch."

Ginny busted out laughing. "Well, cowboy," she said at last, "I can tell you right now you are not the marrying kind. Wade thought he wasn't the marrying kind but he had wedding material written all over him. You, on the other hand…nope. Your granddaddy was really off if he thought he'd marry you off and it would last. It's just going to mess up your dating game for a short while."

"For your information, I don't date much. I haven't found women to be worth the trouble."

Their glares bore into each other. "Well, I can say the same. I haven't found a man yet who makes me feel much. Especially one who makes me feel like getting married."

"I am not surprised."

"Yeah, you're being a smart aleck. It's not going to help your situation any."

"Not going to help your situation any either. From what I hear, you need some money. So I have a proposition for you."

"A proposition?" She started to say something else then stopped. *Oh wow.* "No way."

CHAPTER FOUR

Todd stared at Ginny. She was cute. She had wild brown hair, a nice figure underneath those Western shirts and jeans she was so fond of, and those raggedy old boots she wore a lot. And then there was that hat. Well, he figured he'd seen her twice and she had a hat on both times, always a different color. This one was purple—a hat only a woman would wear. But the purple of the hat made her soft gray eyes look almost lavender but they sparked like storm clouds when she was angry or irritated. He liked her eyes and her hair but not her bossiness and know-it-all attitude.

Once he proposed what he had to say, she was going to be trouble for him. He saw fireworks in his future.

"You know what I'm going to ask. What do you say we join up? I need a wife for three months and three months only, and you need a whole lot of money before the end of four months. I figured we better get hitched quick so by the end of three months you'll have your money."

She stopped chewing her gum. Her expression was that of a woman who thought the person in front of her was talking gibberish. Or a language she didn't understand. He didn't say anything else; he just stared at her and let the clock tick.

After a second, she laughed. "Get out of here. Are you serious?"

"As a heart attack. Because I have a feeling with the two of us together that one of us might end up having one."

"Probably so. But I needed a miracle. I just didn't think it was going to be you."

"Same here. But I can go out and find someone else, if you're not interested. But the longer I drag this out, the longer it will be before I can call that place mine without anything hanging over my head. I figure you got now to decide."

"Well, ain't that mighty nice of you to give me a whole five minutes to decide if I'm going to marry you."

They stared at each other and just like the first time he'd met her, his pulse quickened.

"So, are you going to find all that money you need somewhere else? Because I have a feeling I'm the only miracle that is going to happen to you today. And probably the only miracle that will happen in the next four months. I flew down here with plans to be married tomorrow. I can pull a few strings; we get married and then the clock starts ticking. You could fly back home with me and we can get this thing started."

Her eyes narrowed. "Just like that—you got in a plane and flew down here. I bet you flew down on a private jet?"

He laughed. "Yes, I did. And by the way, this is strictly business—no need to worry about romance."

She hitched a brow. "Good to know you're

thinking straight." She shot two fingers at him and dangled them between her and him. "Because that right there is not happening. You and me—nope, nada. But you're right. You're my only miracle, so I'm all in. I have a feeling we're both going to be in trouble before this deal is over."

He rubbed the bridge of his nose and felt a headache coming on. "On that we agree. But I've got a feeling we're not going to agree on a whole lot of other things."

She held her hand out, knocked her hat back with her other hand so that her eyes were out of the shadow and leveled on him. "Shake on it. I get my money and you get your land and money and whatever else is stipulated in that crazy will of your granddaddy's."

He grinned as he took her hand. A jolt of lightning shot through him and he couldn't help himself; he squeezed her hand and tugged just a little bit so she took a step toward him. "We've got ourselves a deal."

The next day, Ginny stared at the guy she had just

married. They were high in the sky in his little jet. It was cream and tan, and smelled of leather, which had a soft, plush buttery feel to it. It was really nice and felt nothing like any of the commercial planes she had ever flown in. There was a little kitchen and a little bar; there was even a place to sleep in the back. It was really nice but all she could do was stare out the window at the clouds passing by and take a glance at her husband. The cowboy had almost not kissed her at the end of their little marriage ceremony. But then the clerk cleared his throat and said, "You've got to kiss her." And then, as if spurred on by the comment, Todd had wrapped his arm around her waist, pulled her close and planted a kiss on her that had curled her toes. She knew he had done it on purpose, just for spite. He kissed her like a wildfire burning through a Texas drought. His lips met hers and he dug in, and before she knew it, her hands were clenching his shirt and his shoulders and steam was probably coming out of her ears. She hated to say it but she'd enjoyed it.

She had never been kissed much. Only one person had ever caused her heart to race and her world to tilt but that had been a very long time ago. But even that hadn't been like this. Todd McCoy had almost burned her boots off. When he let her go, she stumbled back, catching her breath.

He grinned. "Hello, Mrs. McCoy," he drawled and then he had looked at the clerk, told him thank-you, took her hand and about dragged her out of the courthouse. And she'd let him.

Her parents had been so upset that she was marrying to get the money that they hadn't come to the wedding. She had never been this upset with her parents. It just didn't feel right. Her gaze went over there to Todd. He sat across from her in one of the comfortable seats, leaned back and typing away on his computer. He was a question mark. She couldn't quite figure him out. But as much as he aggravated her, she was very grateful he had shown up when he did. She just wasn't going to tell him that.

The jet was flying over Texas. It was a short, barely a thirty-minute flight for what would have taken him five hours by car. Thank goodness for the luxury jet so that they didn't have time to talk. Not that she had even tried. Obviously, she wasn't ready to talk and he wasn't either.

He was an idiot, he'd kissed her as if she were his love of a lifetime and he needed to prove it to her. And to his surprise, she had kissed him right back. Clutched his shirt and hung on for dear life as she burned his socks off with her kiss. Again, he was an idiot. This was a marriage in name only; there was not supposed to be any of *that* going on. He should've just given her a peck on the lips; that's all he should have done. But no, he had wanted to show her, wanted to tease her with a hot kiss. Only, it had taken on a life of its own. He was going to have to apologize to her and the last thing he wanted to do was apologize to her for anything. Yeah, he was an idiot.

The plane started taking a downward angle and he knew it wouldn't be long before they landed on the airstrip on the back side of the vineyards. And then what? Wade was probably going to meet him there. He wouldn't doubt that Allie was with him. The two of them were gleeful about them getting married. And worried—he knew it—but he had heard a hint of laughter in Wade's voice when he had told him they were going to go through with the wedding and he would be bringing her home on the jet.

He took a deep breath, trying to calm his runaway thoughts. He closed his computer and looked at Ginny. She sat in the chair with her long legs stretched out in front of her and her dusty boots crossed at the ankles. She had worn jeans and boots to the wedding. Kind of had him wondering what she looked like all dressed up. If she ever even *did* dress up. She had her hands clasped together and she looked as if she were about as calm as a cucumber, twiddling her thumbs. But he knew she wasn't; he could see the tension in her shoulders and the set in her jaw. He could feel her looking at him off and on as they flew. He had done his share of looking, too. They were like prize fighters in the ring: him on one side, her on the other. His headache was getting worse.

"We're going to be landing soon."

"No kidding. I felt the plane tip in that direction,

so I assumed we were. You get your work done?"

He deserved that, sitting over there with his mouth shut the whole time. He was a jerk. The woman had married him to help him; he wasn't just doing her a favor and he needed to remember that.

"Look, about the way I acted at the wedding. That kiss. I guess I did it out of meanness."

"Oh, so you're telling me it wasn't my womanly charms that drove you slap crazy and you had to drag me into your arms and kiss me like the world was going to end tomorrow?"

He grinned. *Man, she was something.* "Umm, no, it wasn't that. It was me being a jerk."

"Well, don't stop being it on my account. Because, you know, I can be a jerk myself. And about that kiss—let's not let it happen again."

The woman got under his skin. And he'd deserved every bit of the lashing she'd just given him.

They stared at each other and to his amazement, he wanted to lean across the small distance between them and kiss her again. Yup, he was a glutton for punishment. She was driving him crazy already and they hadn't even landed in Stonewall. Three months—three as in one, two, three—as in *ninety days* he was going to have to deal with her. He wasn't even going to calculate the hours because it wouldn't be good. Not at all.

"Okay then, we've agreed again that we're both jerks. That said, we have to work together. So, look, I know you know a few things about grapes. But I'm pretty good with grapes myself and our McCoy Stonewall Grape Jelly is number one ranked in its class. And our orders have increased—well, the percentage is mind-boggling. So that tells me people are liking what we are doing. And our wine is winning awards. I only say that to let you know that I'd like it if you'd give me a break on telling me how to run my business while you're here. It's not like you're going to come out here and change the way I do things.

"While you're here, just take a little vacation. You're going to be dealing with your other stuff anyway. And by all means, if you need to fly back there for a few days out of every month or week, do so. The will only stipulates you have to be here three weeks out of the month. You know, Wade's contract didn't state that. My granddaddy knew Wade and he knows me, and I guess he must have known who I'd marry—I don't know how—because putting that stipulation in there, he did it to make sure we'd spend time together. But you have seven days to play with out of each month you can go down there and do what you need to do. You can do it all at one time or you can take a little at a time. And we're not staying in the same room. It's a big house."

She was just staring at him and yeah, he was being a jerk again. It was as if he couldn't help himself.

"I'm going to do as much work as I can from here and, just to show you I can hang with you, I'm going to try to not go home at all. So just mark my words, if I go home, it will be because I needed to really badly. It won't be because you ran me off. Got that?"

"Got it." His lip twitched. His pilot let him know on the intercom it was time to put their seat belts on; they would be landing soon. They both buckled up and continued to stare at each other. Thing was, neither one had a poker face on. They were open books. If they'd been standing instead of sitting across from each other, they would be toe to toe, nose to nose, lips to lips right now. *What was he thinking?*

There would not be any more lips to lips in this deal.

None.

"I guess one thing's for sure—the next three months won't be boring."

She laughed and the tension broke. "Nope, I don't think that word has ever been used in association with me." And then she grinned widely, causing a dimple to pop right in the center of her right cheek.

He hadn't seen that dimple before. He hadn't actually seen that smile before. His chest kind of curled up inside in a fuzzy, warm way. Kind of like a kitten pawing on his leg. He decided maybe he didn't need to see that dimple anymore.

He looked out the window and tried to gather his wits about him. "I see Wade and Allie down there." He glanced at her and pointed out his window. She leaned as far over as she could to see out his window and he got a whiff of her peaches-and-cream-smelling hair.

"Oh, I see them," she said, just as the wheels touched the runway. "I'm so glad to see my girl looking so happy."

Ginny was waving her hand across him so Allie could see it in his window. He had leaned back in his chair to give her room. He saw Allie was waving wildly and smiling jubilantly. Wade looked happy and content.

How could these two be best friends? Allie was soft-spoken and quiet sometimes and just not very intrusive. She was like a soothing balm that fit Wade's laid-back charm. And then there was this one. She was a live wire and as intrusive as it got. He didn't see her ever fitting with anybody. Then again, he wasn't a prize right now himself, so he didn't really see himself fitting with nobody either.

Not that he was comparing or thinking he and she could ever fit like Wade and Allie. Oh no. He just couldn't get over Allie and Ginny being buddies. Allie, who probably wouldn't hurt a flea and Ginny, who— Wade had warned him—would probably bring Loretta in her suitcase, if not strapped to her shoulder for all to see. He hadn't seen any sign of Loretta but he had heard she was hot-pink and ready for shooting buckshot at him if the need arose. The idea made him smile. She wouldn't do that. On that, he figured she was all talk but if it got down to it, if someone was messing with her or with Allie or something in particular that was hers, or something she loved, he kind of had a feeling that Ginny wouldn't hesitate.

No, he had to give her credit that if a crisis needed tough action, she was the one he would pick to be on his team if he had to pick somebody other than his brothers. At least, that's the way he figured it right now. She was a protector and he liked that. He liked that part a lot, actually.

But not in a romantic way.

Nope, not that way. Not at all.

The plane was stopped and he shot out of his seat. It was time to get off this plane. Past time. Thankfully, his brother and his new sister-in-law were going to ease some of his stress. He was glad they were here.

"You ready? I think we're going to have dinner with our newlyweds."

Ginny grinned at him. There was challenge in her eyes. She cleared her throat. "Umm, cowboy, I think you're forgetting something. They are here to have dinner with the newlyweds—that'd be you and me. As hard as that is to swallow."

He frowned. "Oh yeah, you're right about that. So all right then, Mrs. McCoy. Let's get this show on the road."

CHAPTER FIVE

Todd stood back and let her exit the plane first. Ginny jogged down the steps and across the short pavement to throw her arms around Allie. "Hello, am I glad to see you."

Allie was laughing as she hugged her tightly. "I'm thrilled you are here. I just can't believe it."

"Me either." Ginny laughed and stepped back.

"We're glad you're here again." Wade gave her a hug.

"Not sure how to answer that myself." She laughed, returning his hug. This cowboy was now her brother-in-law and it felt weird. She really liked Wade and thought he was perfect for her friend. But…her *brother-in-law*? That was a different story. She never in a million or billion years would have dreamed that.

She was going to have to keep her mouth shut at all costs. This was not her patch of grapes; hers were back home and that's all this was about…keeping her vineyard.

"Hey, you two." Todd came up to shake Wade's hand and hug Allie. "Thanks for meeting us. Let's head up to the house. I think lunch is ready."

Wade and Todd grabbed the luggage and loaded it into the back of the black SUV. They all climbed inside and Wade drove them through the vineyard road, toward the big Italian-looking home on the hill. It was amazing.

Ginny studied everything as they passed it. She remembered how beautiful it was from her trip up to visit Allie. But she'd only been here a day; now, she was here for ninety days. And she felt an itch building inside her to play. She loved to play with mixtures. There was an art to making a great bottle of wine and she loved the process.

When they made it to the large, expensive home with wide porches overlooking the vineyards, she stood on the porch and took in the view. This was something she didn't have at her place. They had a small place, with a wooden deck overlooking their vineyards, but their land wasn't rolling and picturesque like this. Hers were straight rows and small. She had to admit, however begrudgingly, that it wasn't as beautiful as this vineyard.

This house would have been out of place at her vineyards, compared to the small building with the wide deck that they had. Why her parents had never grown the vineyards more, she wasn't sure. But a small label could only grow so much and in her heart of hearts, this was what she dreamed of for Rossi Rose of Tyler Wines. But she wouldn't tell Todd McCoy that. She didn't want him to know he had something she longed to have for her own vineyards.

"Don't you just love it here?" Allie looked at her with worry in her eyes. "You're going to be okay, Ginny. You look so tense. I hope you give this a good shot."

"Sure I am," she said, with as much bravado as she could muster. She did not want anyone to know how out of her element she felt right now. Because she did. *Had she gotten in over her head?* The guys were out of earshot. Ginny was not an idiot; she had a feeling Wade was giving Todd a pep talk, too. "Allie, I'm here on business, purely business. So, don't get your hopes up, okay? I'll be going home at the end of three months. Got that?"

Allie sighed. "I've got it. But look—you and Todd at least need to try to get along. Be civil. I know that something between y'all doesn't agree, but if you could put down your barriers for just a little while, I think you two would like each other. He's a nice guy and you're a great gal, and if you would get past trying to tell him how to run his vineyard and be amicable, you would have the love of vineyards in common."

Ginny dipped her chin and gave her beloved friend a give-me-a-break look.

Allie flattened her lips, dipped her own chin and continued, "Yes, he's got some prickly thorns sticking off him, but no more than you. He's got a lot on his mind and maybe he's got some things in his past or in his heart that we don't know about and he doesn't want to expose himself by getting too close to anyone. Kind of like you." She added the last bit in a hushed voice because she knew how touchy Ginny was on that subject. Only Allie knew the secret Ginny carried in her heart. The ache that never went away.

"Don't go there," she muttered.

"I'm not, but I'm just sayin' you could try to be friends while you are here. I'm not going to that other heart issue. But you know you're hurting over what your parents did and you could use a friend. He's hurting too."

"Allie, I don't have any issues in my heart, especially over that. I'm just mad and I'm going to fix it, buy my vineyard from my parents, and live happily ever after in Tyler, Texas at Rossi Rose Vineyard."

"You can tell me that but I don't completely believe you. I know you're hurting inside at the thought that you could lose it. But this is your answer and it is a miracle. So just relax. I know when I came here that's what everyone kept telling me—relax, use it as a vacation. I was so eaten up with grief and worry and stress and overwork and yet, well, I couldn't even imagine I could relax, but I did. And you know, for the first time in my life, I gave myself permission to be the person I always wanted to be. The one who wasn't weighed down by all the other stuff—okay, this is not about me. It's about you. And you've got walls up, Ginny—big, thick, high walls up around that heart of yours. I'm not saying you've got to let them down and get all vulnerable and weepy-eyed and emotional, but at least crack that door open a little bit and give that poor guy some room. At least don't have a war with him."

Ginny inhaled, feeling her chest tighten. Allie knew her but that didn't mean she was going to do what Allie wanted. She couldn't. And that was that. At least on the opening her heart part. It hurt too bad to open her heart. And she couldn't even imagine ever having to go through the kind of heartache she had frozen deep inside her heart.

An older woman wearing a button-down white

shirt and dark slacks with a long gray ponytail curled into a bun at the back of her neck came into the room. "Dinner is served," she said.

"Mavis has dinner cooked," Wade called.

They came over and he opened the door to the house.

Todd slipped his hat off, exposing his wavy hair. The man was so good-looking that she felt a pang of aggravation at it, especially considering her fingers— the traitors—wanted to run through his thick waves and see whether they felt as amazing as they looked. *Oh, brother, she was so in trouble.* This was a dilemma she preferred not to have on top of everything else.

She reiterated a warning to herself: *there wasn't going to be any attraction to her temporary husband at all, no, ma'am, so she could just back off now.* To show herself she had what it took to ignore these urges of attraction she was feeling toward him, she let her eyes move to him. He was watching her and her pulse instantly shot sky-high.

He came to stand beside her. "Mavis, I'd like to introduce you to Ginny, my wife."

He said the words so easily that it shocked her. She stared at him, stunned, then caught herself and forced her gaze to the older woman, who had approached with a broad smile on her face.

"Hello, Mavis. It's nice to meet you," she managed, and held her hand out.

"I am so glad to meet you. When Todd texted me to let me know he'd married, I didn't know the particulars but I was thrilled. This place needs a mistress and you look," she grinned and took in Ginny's clothing, from her Western shirt to her jeans and scuffed boots, "like you will fit on this vineyard. I have a feeling you are a hands-on kind of woman and that's what it takes. But don't you worry, I will cook as long as you want me to if you prefer to be outside. Or if you want to be in the kitchen, you just let me know what suits you. I'm easy. Goodness knows this big place has enough to keep me busy."

Ginny smiled, feeling at ease with the good-natured lady. "You're right, I'm a hands-on kind of gal. I do like the kitchen sometimes, but I think I will love not having to deal with meals."

"Perfect. Well, let's get in there and chow down. I've got chicken cordon bleu and a salad, and I took the liberty of making a small wedding cake. I wasn't sure if y'all were going to have a wedding reception like Penny threw for Wade and Allie, so I went ahead and did one. I do love to bake special cakes."

They all started to follow her through the house toward the room she had come from. Ginny had not been inside the house until now and she was in awe.

It was amazing: Tall ceilings with huge log beams. A wide-open living area with thick couches adorned with reds and grays and tans and bold colors. Rugs covered sections of the fabulous tiled floors. The furniture was bold; it looked exactly like what she would picture in a beautiful winery's visitation room or tasting room.

She paused and looked at Todd. "Is this your tasting room?"

"We do use it for big parties. We have a smaller tasting room on the west wing area that's a normal-size tasting room, where we have workers every day. Having people in this part of the house is not my favorite thing but this room was built for that, so it's utilized when needed. We're going into the main living space and the public isn't allowed past this door."

He held the door and she walked past him into a smaller version of what they'd just come from.

"This is an amazing house." She followed, eager to see the rest.

"Thanks. It's big. So, you'll have to get used to where everything is." Todd led the way through the room with its wide windows that overlooked the vineyard. This room had plush leather couches, a huge television on the wall, and a monster of a fireplace.

They continued on into a dining room, where Mavis had dinner set up.

Ginny entered the room first and stepped to the side as Allie came in behind her and then the guys. She gasped. The table was massive. Some kind of wood table—she wasn't exactly sure what: oak or teak or spruce—pecan, whatever, it was beautiful and there were twelve chairs around it with seat cushions in cream and grape tones. The table was set elegantly, with cloth napkins pulled through gold napkin rings and placed across a salad plate sitting inside a dinner plate. And enough silverware surrounded the beautiful dishes for several people to use. It was a very formal setting and crystal goblets were at the ready.

She would have made a snappy remark that it was a bit too formal for her taste but Mavis stood at the head of the table, waiting for them to come in and take their seats. The woman had obviously meant to welcome Ginny with this lavish display and there was no way Ginny could say anything that would hurt the woman's feelings. After today, surely things would not be this formal.

As if sensing her thoughts, Allie said softly, "Isn't it lovely?" She gave Ginny a look that said *Say something nice*. Ginny knew Allie's looks well, and Allie knew hers too.

"It is awesome," she said. "Mavis, you've gone way above and beyond what I could have imagined. Thank you. But please don't go to this much trouble in the future for me."

"Mr. Todd wanted you to feel welcomed and so did I, so we're celebrating today," she said, kindly.

"We'll be more down-to-earth after this. How's that?"

She liked this woman. "Perfect. Because I am as down-to-earth as it gets."

Todd had planned this? She did not miss that fact. The man was full of surprises.

"I'll be right back with the food," she said, and turned to walk away.

"Can I help you?" Ginny asked, starting to stand.

"No, thank you, I'll bring it in," Mavis said, then walked away to get the food.

Todd grinned. "Mavis lets you know when she needs help and when she doesn't. She has a big line in red permanent marker around her duties and she insists no one cross the line. I just go with the flow. She can be a pill when she's riled up. You two should get along fine."

She gave him a droll look. "So she tries to keep you in line?"

He laughed. "Not exactly. She just gives me a hard time sometimes. Doesn't mean it fazes me."

"I figured that."

Wade and Allie were watching them.

Allie frowned. "Maybe you two should call a truce for now. It's going to be a long three months if you don't."

Mavis returned with the food on a rolling cart and they passed each bowl and plater around, each of them taking what they wanted and then setting the dishes on the center of the table. Ginny used this time to decide to keep her mouth shut.

Picking up her fork and knife, she cut a portion of her chicken, and then took a big bite. It was her safest bet to keeping her mouth shut. *If this was what it would take*... Mavis's cooking was delicious. She was going to gain at least ten pounds before she headed back home.

CHAPTER SIX

After dinner, Todd thought Ginny looked tired, though he was pretty sure if he said something about it, she would tell him she wasn't. Todd figured carrying around that chip on her shoulder—or whatever it was—wore her out. He had begun to wonder whether the girl ever let up. She had steel bars erected around herself that were so tightly wound around her that he figured she probably couldn't breathe.

And the thing was, he had begun to wonder what it would be like to slowly tear those iron bars down so she could escape whatever it was that made her like that. Then again, it could just be that she did not like him.

But he had a suspicion it was more than that, more even than her parents selling her beloved vineyard.

Not that she would agree with him that she had any bars. The woman wanted everyone, especially him, to think that she had no soft points about her. She thought she had to be tough all the time. Surely there was something in there soft. Despite everything she tried to hide, he knew she had a soft spot for Allie. It was completely evident. And if she had one soft spot, it meant there were more; they were just behind those bars she was hiding behind.

And why he was wondering all of this, he had no clue. Especially when he knew trying to soften her up could get him into a lot of trouble. But she was a challenge and he had never been able to resist a challenge.

Everything about Ginny Rossi challenged him. *McCoy.* He reminded himself that she was now his wife. Her attitude alone was challenging enough but he could not fight off the attraction he felt toward her. And that kiss…man, oh man, he could not get it off his mind. He needed to keep away. This was a business deal.

They stood beside each other on the porch and watched Allie and Wade walk happily, arm in arm, to their vehicle. Todd waved at them; she did, too, and then watched them drive down the drive toward the exit of the vineyards.

He glanced at Ginny. "They got really lucky finding each other."

"Yes, they did."

The sun was going down over the vineyard and a golden glow was cast over the long rows of grapes. She studied the view. "It's really pretty here."

"I think so."

She sighed then rubbed her temple and he saw a flicker of sadness in her eyes.

He felt bad for her. "I guess you miss your vineyard?"

She turned to him. "Yes, I do. I'm tired. If you'll show me where my room is, I'll get out of your hair."

She admitted she was tired; he had gotten that wrong. "Well, of course, Mrs. McCoy. I'll be glad to show you to your room. Anything I can do for you?"

Her eyes narrowed. "Not one thing, cowboy."

He laughed. "This way." He headed down the hallway. She followed—at a distance, he noted. At her door, he pushed it open. "This will be yours, so if you get scared during the night, since it's such a big house, or if you need anything, just knock on my door it's right there." He pointed to the door directly across from hers. He grinned and hitched a brow of invitation. Just to rile her up, but also, he noted only to himself, that he wouldn't turn her away.

Ginny stared at the door and then at him, her gaze dropping to his grin. And then she glared at him.

"I won't be coming in or knocking. You can just get that thought out of your mind."

His grin widened. She was so fun to tease and he could push her buttons so easy; it was too tempting. He wondered whether she had any idea how easy she was to read. "What if I get scared? Can I knock on your door?"

She gave him a very direct look. "I've got Loretta in there with me. She rode in my suitcase."

He did a salute and winked. "Got your message loud and clear, my dear. I'll see you in the morning. Since obviously, I won't be seeing you any time before that."

"Don't know why you even expected anything other than that."

"Oh, I didn't. But then, I *sure* do like pushing your buttons." He opened his door and walked inside before she could reply. He liked pushing her buttons a little bit more than was comfortable. He knew he was going to really have to watch himself.

Two days after she'd arrived at the vineyard, Ginny was ready to spit nails. Todd McCoy loved to yank her chain. And every time he did, she took the bait. It was ridiculous. She knew what he was doing; she knew good and well what he was doing, and yet every time he said something that got to her, she had to say something back—which was just what he wanted.

They couldn't agree on much of anything, so most of the time they weren't talking. Or they were bickering, like now.

"You are wasting all these grapes on jelly? I cannot fathom this, I keep thinking I misunderstood you from when I was here visiting Allie when she first married Wade. This isn't a vineyard—it's been reduced to a grape farm. And that's just sad. You should use all of these quality grapes for wines. Just think of the new wines you could produce. Then it would be a vineyard. I had no idea the jelly was the majority of your business."

"I like my jelly business. You're a wine snob. And this is a vineyard, despite that I make the bulk of my money from jelly."

"I'm not a snob. I just prefer using all these luscious grapes to produce wine. Do you really make the bulk of your money from the jelly?" It was bothering him that she wouldn't call his vineyard a vineyard because he made grape jelly.

"I do. And for your information, I make a lot of money from the wine, even more so from Stonewall

Grape Jelly. Our wine is good. Our grapes are healthy. Our soil is perfect. Our label is bigger than yours and still, our jelly is bigger."

"Really?"

"McCoy Stonewall Jelly is all over the country and we're going international. I've worked my butt off to get it that way."

"And you forsook your wine in the meantime."

"What is your problem? Just because I prefer jelly to wine, it irritates you. I happen to not be as big a fan of wine as I am jelly. I do like me some great, grape jelly on my biscuit."

She laughed, taking in his trim, fit form—more than she wanted to. She wasn't sure where he stored all the carbohydrates from the biscuits he claimed he ate all the time with the sugary jelly on it. Unable to help herself, she gave in—for the moment, anyway. "Fine. Guess what, dearest, darling husband of mine," she said with a heavy dose of teasing sarcasm. "I'll have to cook breakfast for you and make sure you have some of my homemade biscuits on the table."

He got this funny look on his face. "You cook?"

She frowned. "Um, yes. Why, you don't think a girl like me can cook?"

"Honestly, no."

She glared at him. "You do like to misjudge people, don't you? I'll have you know I'm probably one of the best cooks you'll ever come across. And my biscuits—oh, you have not tasted a biscuit until you taste my biscuits."

He grinned widely. "Well, darling wife of mine, I look forward to that. You are welcome in my kitchen anytime. Why don't you go in there and make some right now? You bring on the biscuits, I'll bring the jelly."

She laughed. "You think you are so smart. You think just because you challenged me that I'm going to march in there and make those biscuits."

He grinned. "You are."

They stared at each other...and he had that irritating little twitch to his lips. She wanted to smack him one. She wanted to kiss him. And that just made her want to smack herself.

"Ohhh, you make me so mad," she huffed. "I'm

not going to go do it right now but I am going to make you some biscuits. Mark my word, you're going to pass out."

"Well, darlin', if they're going to be that good, I may just have to haul you over my shoulder and carry you in there right now and set you down in front of the oven."

She got a picture of him hauling her into the kitchen over his shoulder. That might be kind of fun, actually. *Smack herself again*, she thought. "Don't you dare."

He grinned wider. "You daring me?"

She took a step back. "I'm saying, don't you dare pick me up."

He took a step forward.

She snapped her hand into the middle of his chest. "You will be so sorry if you do this."

Next thing she knew, the grinning son of a gun swished her up into his arms and she was kicking and screaming as he strode through his grape patch toward the big house.

She pounded on his back. "You put me

down...you, you big brute."

He chuckled. His warm hands were on her legs and she had to put her hands on his back to stop herself from slamming her face against his shoulder blades.

"Let me down."

"Hey, you said you wanted to make me some biscuits and you dared me to do this. I have a feeling you and me both feel the same way about challenges and dares—we cannot resist them."

She quit struggling. The guy was right and she had fallen for his craziness once more. "You think you're so smart. What makes you think now I'm not going to mess up those biscuits?"

He patted her on the rump once and she slapped him on the back.

"Your pride's not going to let you mess up those biscuits."

She closed her eyes and gritted her teeth. "You're right. But mark my words, cowboy—you've got one coming somewhere, sometime. I'm going to get back at you for this."

"*Darlin'*—I look forward to it."

CHAPTER SEVEN

When they reached the kitchen, Todd yanked a chair out from the table with his boot and plopped Ginny down on that chair. He put his hands on his hips and grinned at her. He had enjoyed that.

Of course, she had kicked him once in the hip and he got a little bit worried that if she kept kicking so hard she'd hurt him, but thankfully she'd stopped kicking.

He felt a little bit as if he had just wrangled a calf. But she was a whole lot prettier than any calf. This was not something he normally did with a woman, but he hadn't been able to resist.

Now she glared at him. "If I was a little bit bigger, I'd haul you over my shoulder then chuck you out there in the cow manure."

He laughed, finding her extremely entertaining. "Wouldn't be anything I haven't felt before, though you'd have to carry me over to the ranch to find a pile of manure."

"Of course, when I need a pile it's nowhere to be found within reach." She crossed her arms.

"So how about those biscuits?"

Her brows dipped and he figured she was contemplating what she could find to poison his biscuits with.

"If you really can make amazing biscuits. Jury's still out on that."

"You are so irritating. Since it's almost lunchtime, I guess I could whip up a batch. But don't start thinking I'm going to begin cooking your lunch every day."

"Don't worry—most days I'm not around the house enough to eat lunch here. That's why Mavis takes the middle of the day off. But you know, it's pretty sweet when my wife wants to cook for me, so I'll just be glad to come over here and eat anything you want to cook. Especially if it's as good as you say it is."

She shook her head and didn't take the bait. Instead, she went to the pantry, opened the door, and walked inside the large area. "Wow. You could feed an army from here."

"Mavis keeps it stocked."

"I see that. You've got the flour on one shelf then you've got the sugar sitting down there in the corner of the bottom shelf."

"So now you don't like the way my pantry is organized?"

"Forget it. I'm just visiting inside your pantry, so I'm going to keep my mouth shut."

He laughed. "I'll believe that when I hear it."

"You watch, I'm not going to tell you that you need to prune your vines a little better either."

"See? Couldn't do it. I've been waiting for you to tell me that all morning. Same thing you told me last time you were here. I prune my vines exactly like they need to be pruned. We do a really good job with that."

"No. It's sloppy. They'd do so much better. And your grafting is wrong."

"You're wrong."

"I am not. Now you know we're going to disagree on this, so I'm going to make you your biscuits and you'll bring the jelly."

"Can't have biscuits and jelly without bacon. Are you going to make me some bacon?"

"I didn't say anything about making bacon."

He grinned at her. She was sassy. "Then I'll make the bacon. I've got the best bacon in the country."

"Boy, is that a statement to make. You telling me you raise your own pigs?"

"Actually, no, but my cousins do. And they know how to raise hogs."

"You know, I'm not thrilled to talk about hogs turning into bacon."

"I hate to tell you this, but those hogs and those cows that my brother and my cousins raise feed the world pretty much. They're the mainstay of the food chain."

"I know that. Still, I don't want to talk about the pigs and hogs turning into bacon. But if you want to make me some good bacon, I'll eat it. Because you're right, if we are going to have biscuits and jelly, we need bacon and eggs. I'll make the biscuits and scramble the eggs while you fry the bacon."

"Sounds like a plan."

And with that, they both went to work. He went to the refrigerator, pulled out the bacon, and pulled out the pan he liked to fry it up in. He set it on one of the six burners on the gas stove. He was glad it was a big one because they needed their space, that was for certain. He eyed her from the corner of his eyes as he watched her gather up all of her supplies on the granite island in the middle of the big kitchen. She was prissy and cute and he had a hard time not watching her.

He wasn't going to tell her that, or let her see him sneaking peeks either. He figured she wouldn't like being called prissy or being watched. But he couldn't help himself.

"Sure are looking good over there, darlin'." He

smiled, knowing every time he called her darlin' it probably irritated the fire out of her.

"Honey bunch, you're looking good over there, too, frying up that bacon."

"I'm not frying yet but you just wait. It's going to get hot in here when I do and you're going to be asking me on a hot date."

She laughed so hard that he got a little bit embarrassed. He turned toward her. She was staring at him. "What's so funny?"

"You are so full of it, mister. Believe me, if and when I go looking for a hot date, it's not going to be somebody I can barely stand."

"Something tells me that's not exactly true, the you not standing me part."

"Oh, it's true. Your ego just won't let you believe it."

"No. I can tell you like me."

"I do not. Besides, you don't like me." She shot him a hitched brow to match his own.

He liked her a lot. The thought slammed him in the face. Where did that thought come from? No, she

77

was fun to tease but he did not like her, not like that. No sir, no *siree*—not like that.

"I've got to fry this bacon up." He spun back to the bacon and went to work. She probably went back to making biscuits. Thankfully, the room got quiet for a little while. But his brain wasn't quiet; his brain kept going over that statement inside his head.

He did not like her like *that*.

CHAPTER EIGHT

Ginny was highly disturbed by the aggravating attraction she felt toward Todd. She rolled out the dough for her biscuits and she did it just like her grandmother had always taught her. Her sweet grandmother, who had always told her it would take a special man to make her fall in love. She'd say, "Ginny, honey, don't you ever settle. Do you hear me, now? You got a wild spirit and a temperament that knows exactly what you want. Don't you let no man come along and try to tamp that down. No, ma'am. You grow up and you be yourself. And if a man doesn't like it, you just let him march right out of your life. You understand me, honey?"

Ginny let those words flow through her as she worked with that biscuit dough. Her sweet granny had, at some point, had a spirit like Ginny's. But her grandmother had given up a lot to make Ginny's grandfather happy. She had given up dreams, given up her spirit. She had had to get married at an early age because she had gotten pregnant with Ginny's daddy. She loved Ginny's daddy with all her heart. And she wouldn't have given him up for anything. Her granny had never regretted, not one day, the choices that she made. But she wanted Ginny to marry a man she loved with all of her heart. She wished Ginny wouldn't give herself to anyone before she was married and before she was old enough to know what she was doing. And Ginny had listened to her grandmother.

She did have a wild tendency, but she had loved her grandmother like she had loved no one else and she had sworn she would never ever, ever make any kind of mistake that would cause her to lose her dreams. And Ginny believed in her heart of hearts that if she could make her dreams come true, she would also be making her grandma's dreams come true. Unexpected tears came to her eyes as she placed the biscuits on a baking tray.

She glanced over her shoulder, making sure Todd wasn't looking; he was busy frying the bacon. She looked back at her biscuits and dabbed at her eyes. She would not cry in front of anyone, especially him. When was the last time she had teared up, anyway? One thing her granny wouldn't want was her crying over her. Her granny had raised her to be strong and independent. Of course, it hadn't taken much; like her granny said, she had been born strong and independent.

Thankfully, her parents had been glad she was, too. Although they had been scared to death during her high school years that she was out being involved in mischief if ever she was out late with a boy. But she wasn't. Matter of fact, there had been rumors about her, rumors that had been hard to live down after a guy had tried to hold her down and force himself on her. She knew how to kick and fight like a wildcat and she'd hurt him. But she hadn't stopped there; she had threatened him with Loretta if he ever touched her. She and Loretta went way back. Matter of fact, it had been her grandma who had told her Loretta would be her best friend at some point in her life.

And Loretta had been. But nothing could stop the rumors that the jerk started about her. And from that night on, her reputation had been shot. A reputation that Allie, bless her heart, had never believed.

All she had to do was tell Allie it was a lie and Allie had believed her. Not one other soul had ever believed her. Not even her mother and her dad. From that ridiculous day forth, her parents had believed the worst of her—well, not the worst, but they believed she had lied to them and they had been worried for weeks that she would show up pregnant.

She and Allie knew that would have been a true miracle. She hadn't thought about all that in so long. Problem was, after what that guy said, every time she thought a guy might be interested in her, she'd go on a date and find out that he had heard the rumors and thought she was easy. So, she had quit going out.

Hadn't taken long before she decided everybody

in her high school was no good. And then Kyle had come along and proved her wrong. He had moved to town and taken her breath away. He was so gorgeous and nice. It had taken awhile for her to believe he could be as nice as he seemed. It had taken even longer for him to coax her into going out on that date with him. When she agreed at last, she had been a nervous wreck because she feared he would prove to be like the rest of them. But he hadn't been. No, he had been the real deal. He laughed when she got bossy; he had teased her relentlessly and he had broken down her emotional barriers. And he respected her when she told him no.

And she had known that if she told him that what the others said about her was not true, that he would go tearing down some walls and hurt somebody, because he was that kind of hero. So, she hadn't told him. No, she had told him that she had changed. That she had realized that misbehaving like she had been doing was a one-way street to nowhere and that one reason she hadn't dated in so long was because she had changed.

He had believed her. Then he had graduated and

immediately joined the Marines; he was gone with promises to be back.

Only he hadn't made it back. He'd been a hero and saved the others around him when he had thrown himself on top of a grenade. Just because that was the kind of guy that he was.

Ginny had never forgotten him.

It had been four years. She hadn't dated a soul and she didn't plan on it. She hadn't planned on ever getting married. She wasn't ever, ever going to lose her heart to someone again. What was the use of giving your heart to someone, only to have it ripped out of you? It just wasn't worth it.

She realized she had been lost in thought. *What in the world was coming over her?* She wiped the tears off her cheeks, hoping Todd thought that it looked as though she were wiping flour off her face.

"I tell you, this making biscuits gets flour all over a person." She hoped he didn't hear the emotional edge to her voice. She yanked up her big girl panties and tossed her memories to the curb. And then she cleaned up her mess without looking at him again.

He hadn't said anything. He was over there, frying up that bacon and concentrating. When she felt as if maybe her face wasn't revealing anything, she picked up the leftover dough and made a small biscuit and added it to the pan. "I'll be right back. I have to run to the restroom."

She needed to look at her face and wipe it clean. Make sure her eyes weren't red. Give herself time to get these crazy emotions under control. When she reached the bathroom, she saw that her eyes were a little bit red so she tossed water on her face then soaked a cloth in cold water and held it to her eyes and face.

It had been awhile since she had made biscuits. But biscuits didn't normally make her cry. She didn't know why today of all days her grandma's words came to her, bringing back all these memories. She was going back out there now and she would be her old, tough self. The last person she wanted thinking she was an emotional basket case was Todd McCoy.

CHAPTER NINE

Todd watched Ginny leave the room. He was almost thinking he had heard her voice wobble, as if she were crying. It was hard for him to believe but he was almost certain of it. *But why?*

Surely, him teasing her by carrying her in here like a sack of potatoes hadn't made her cry. Not Ginny. But then what? All she had been doing was making biscuits. And she'd gotten really quiet all of a sudden; he'd looked over to see what she was doing and that's when he saw her swiping at her cheeks. All he could see was her back but then she'd spoken and he'd heard the wobble.

He wanted to think he was imagining things. But he didn't think so.

She came back into the room with a smile on her face. "You haven't taken my biscuits out of the oven yet, have you?" Walking over to the oven, she looked through the window. "They're rising."

His second batch of bacon was frying happily in the pan, so he leaned against the counter, crossed his arms and watched her. "I'm letting you do these biscuits because if they're as good as you say they are, I'm not going to do anything to mess them up. My bacon is almost done. Are you sure you don't want me to do the eggs? I don't mind."

"No, I've got the eggs." She strode over to the refrigerator, pulled open the door, grabbed a batch of eggs and brought them back over to the counter.

"You looking for a bowl?"

She shot a glance at him. "Yes. Any ideas?"

"Right there, past your left leg—bottom shelf."

She pulled the door open to the bottom cabinet, bent down and pulled out a red mixing bowl. Her jeans stretched tight across her backside and he decided maybe he needed to watch the bacon instead of her. He picked his fork up and started to turn the bacon over.

He heard her cracking the eggs next to him. Silence stretched between them. He reminded himself sternly that he didn't need any romantic ideas about Ginny. *He wasn't that stupid, was he?*

He wasn't sure what she was thinking but he was pretty sure she would laugh if she knew what he was thinking about.

They had been on the edge of flirting during some of their conversations. They had slipped over that line into flirting and even teasing with ease, and that was disturbing. If it disturbed him, he knew it disturbed her.

Feeling torn by what he was thinking and feeling, he carried the plate of hot bacon to the kitchen island and set it down. As he walked over to grab the napkins and the dinnerware, he realized he should have asked her how she liked her bacon fried. She was dishing up the eggs and he had to reach past her to open the cabinet with the plates. His shoulder brushed hers as he picked the plates out of the cabinet. She turned her head slightly and their eyes met. He froze and she didn't move. He could've sworn there was vulnerability swirling in the depths of her eyes that he had not seen before.

"Uh, I needed to get the plates."

"I see that. Put them on the island over there and I'll get the biscuits." There was a tightness to her voice.

He wanted to ask her why her eyes looked different. Why was there a softness in them now? Or sadness? *What did Ginny have to be sad about?* She wasn't losing her vineyard any longer; she should be happy. They were saving it through this fiasco of a marriage.

His gaze dropped to her lips. He felt an undeniable, strong desire to kiss her. *No kissing.* Especially while wondering whether she'd been crying. *Had he made her cry?*

He grabbed the plates and stepped back so fast that he was glad he didn't stumble and fall. "I'll put these on the island." He repeated her directions, like a fool.

Her eyes sparked, looking more alive. "Don't fall down, cowboy."

She sounded normal, thank goodness. He was not good at this emotional stuff. "You're just saying that because you don't want to have to clean up this glass if I break it. Not even worried about my bones."

"I have a feeling your bones are strong enough and too stubborn to break anyway. But I don't want to clean up the blood if you cut yourself."

He laughed. "Well, nothing like being truthful anyway."

"Exactly. Now, time to eat."

"Hallelujah." He needed a fantastic biscuit to take his mind off Ginny.

He went to the refrigerator, pulled out a jar of McCoy Stonewall Grape Jelly, and popped the lid on it. Then he straddled the barstool beside Ginny and smiled at her.

Ginny set the biscuits on the granite island. They smelled out of this world. And they were beautiful. Tall and perfectly round and golden, she had swiped butter across them so they glistened and his mouth watered. He did love a good biscuit.

"I was going to say taste and be amazed when I set my jelly on the counter, but I'm looking at those biscuits and if they taste as good as they look, I'll be the one to be amazed."

"Actually, it could end up being that when we combine the two of them, they're a perfect match and we are both amazed. I learned from my grandma how to make my heavenly biscuits, which is the only reason I could take pride in them because nobody could make biscuits or cinnamon rolls like my grandma. We baked biscuits until she felt I could bake them just as good as hers. I'm proud of that fact. Now, if that jelly is a good match for them, boy, we're going to be in heaven here in just a minute."

He smiled at her, liking the way she thought. "I hate to say this, but I'm kind of hoping that I agree with you and in that case, would we have found a point that we are mutually agreeing on? And I'm hoping for some cinnamon rolls sometime."

She gave him an expression that told him that she

might not want to concede to the point. It was cute.

"Maybe so," she said at last. "But don't get used to it."

He held his hands up. "I would never."

They spent the next few minutes buttering biscuits and filling their plates with eggs that smelled fabulous and had some little green specks in them. She had chopped up some green onion to put in them, but he didn't know what spice she had been using because he didn't look when she was adding them. "What's that spice you've got on these eggs?"

"A little basil. I love basil and it's really good for you."

"Basil? That's not one I use a lot. Of course, as I told you, I don't do a lot of cooking."

"When Mavis isn't here, say, when she's on vacation, do you starve?"

"Are you kidding? She has food in the freezer ready to defrost and bake. It would feed me for weeks. Especially since I go to Dixie's Diner most of the time, or, sometimes I take the jet and have dinner with friends."

She stared at him. "You take the jet. You say that like you're taking the car and driving to town for dinner."

He looked sheepish. "I don't do it all the time, but I will admit that on occasion I do. If you'd like, I can take you somewhere nice for dinner." He said it with caution because he really didn't know how she would react to the suggestion.

She looked perplexed. "I can't imagine being able to do that."

He picked up a biscuit. "Don't imagine it—tell me where you want to go to dinner and we'll go."

She laughed. "Maybe later. I'm still adjusting to being here right now."

"Then I'll take you to Dixie's. It's right there in Stonewall and it's great. But I have to tell you, her breakfast doesn't smell like this. And her biscuits...she has good biscuits but they don't look like these."

She buttered one for him and took the one he was holding as she replaced it with the buttered one. Her touch distracted him and he was thinking about her lips again.

She scooted the jelly toward him. "Take a little

try."

He yanked his thoughts back to reality. "Don't mind if I do." He put jelly on that biscuit and a little bit more butter; then, holding it with both hands, he bit into it.

An explosion of buttery biscuit melted in his mouth and it mingled with the sweetness of the jelly he was so proud of. *Oh yeah, this was amazing.*

"Mmm, you make a good biscuit," he mumbled, as he took another bite.

She crossed her arms and grinned. "Told you."

He nodded at her, not willing to talk now as he was just going to finish eating the biscuit and enjoy every crumb.

"I'm glad you like it but I knew you would." She picked up a piece of bacon and bit into it and watched him.

His chest tightened as he looked at her. "Darlin', I could marry you for these biscuits."

She laughed. "Well, don't forget—we're already married."

He grinned. "How could I forget?"

CHAPTER TEN

Ginny liked the area. She liked the jelly business. She was really surprised by that. Jelly compared to wine—she had always enjoyed winemaking and still favored it but she got why he liked the jelly, especially considering it was so successful.

She wasn't a huge drinker but she still loved the process of producing wine. She thrilled at getting the mixture just right and coming up with a perfect blend to bottle. From concept to the table for a buyer, she loved it.

But when she walked into the jelly factory—or, as

Todd referred to it, the "house of happiness"—he talked about the process of making jelly in the same way she talked about making wine. She smiled, remembering him telling her his nickname for the building. His smile had warmed her; it was boyish and mischievous at the same time.

She had to admit that she had never thought about how getting the recipe right for jelly was also a challenge. He had a testing room, a large production area, and of course, an area where they tested new recipes. It was a huge setup.

And all the people who worked there were really friendly and seemed to enjoy their jobs. And they liked Todd. She had to admit the cowboy had grown on her. When she wasn't giving him a hard time about not tending his vineyard the way she tended hers, he wasn't sarcastic or irritating. It was getting harder and harder not to keep her guard up around him. The biscuit episode hadn't helped.

Today, he had introduced her around as his wife and that felt weird. But that's what she was—at least, for the moment. In the tasting room, there were two older women working and they perked up like peacocks the moment she was introduced.

"We've been wondering when this was going to happen, who the lucky girl was going to be," said the redheaded lady. She wore bright-red lipstick that clashed with her orange-red hair. And her blue eyes sparkled as she smiled at Ginny and Todd.

The other lady had beautiful, caramel-colored skin and black hair with tiny specks of gray showing up in it. "I've been tellin' y'all he was going to get married. No man could look that good and not get married. Some girl was going to snag you right up, that's what I told you. Isn't it, Todd?"

He laughed, looking embarrassed. "Yes, Ethel, you did."

"I told you that too," the redhead said. "Me and Ethel discuss this a lot. And now that you've brought this pretty little gal in here, I'm just really excited. And I like that cowgirl hat. Matter of fact, I'll trade you this hair net for it right now."

Ginny swept her baby-blue hat off her head and held it out to the lady. "Be my guest. I brought a suitcase full of them. I do like color when it comes to a hat."

"Well I do, too, girl." She took the hat. "By the way, my name is Clara."

"I'm glad to meet you, Clara, and you, too, Ethel."

"Sorry I didn't get official introductions done before y'all started talking. But it was kind of hard." His teasing expression brought laughter to Clara and Ethel.

"Ha, like you ever can get many words in when we're around," Ethel said.

He laughed. "Truer words were never spoken. Now, before y'all get started again, I'm going to take Ginny and show her around. As always, y'all are doing an awesome job."

"You know flattery will get you everywhere." Clara giggled. "And you're looking mighty beautiful doing it."

He winked at them.

Ethel slapped him on the arm. "You old flirting fool—you go flirt with your wife. Go on now."

He laughed and slipped his arm around Ginny's

shoulders and led her toward the doors. He leaned close to her ear and whispered, "They keep this place running like a jewel. You wouldn't be able to find two better women in all the world."

Ginny looked at him. She was very aware of his arm on her shoulders but she figured he was doing that as a show for the ladies. She felt a little bit underhanded for that. They were close to him and they were deceiving them. But she liked that he could tease them so easily. She realized that as hardnosed as he seemed when she met him, he did like to tease. She had definitely figured that out. "They look like they enjoy their job."

"I try to make sure everybody likes their job. Just makes life easier, don't you think?"

"It makes life a whole lot easier. That's why I like my wine making so much. And I can see why you like this too. Honestly, you have a little bit of both worlds. I'm eager to see your winery. Not that I'm not eager to see this—your jelly making is extraordinary."

He gave her a squeeze and then let go as they walked into the next room. "Just wait until you get to the testing room. We will have a few samples. Dan, who's overseeing that, knows jelly. And he tests flavors all the time. Even though we have our traditional winning flavor, we're getting ready to come out with a few new flavors. They're all delicious."

She stopped walking and just stared at him. "For a big, strong, muscular, tough guy like you, I would have never, in all my imagination, believed you to be a jelly maker. But you love it."

He grinned and waggled his eyebrows. "Just teaches you not to judge a fellow by his appearance. Although, I have to say I like that you think I'm a big, strong, muscular-looking man. But don't you think being a jelly maker gives me a sweeter side?"

She laughed and pushed his shoulder. "I think it makes you full of it, Dude."

"Well, now that we're clear about all that...let's go in here and you can tell me just how wonderful I am after you get to taste all these amazing jellies. Only thing I can think of that would make them taste better is having them on your wonderful biscuits. You are going to make me some more biscuits, right? I mean honestly, I'll do whatever I need to in order to get some more biscuits."

"Show me your wine and I'll make you some biscuits. Now, what am I going to taste this jelly on in here? Surely I'm not going to have to eat spoonfuls of this sweet stuff by itself. Because that's just yuck."

"We've got crackers and bread and all kinds of things in here for you to taste it on. We have to make sure we know what it's going to taste like on other things. And there's biscuits in here, too, just not your biscuits."

The man was incorrigible. And she was going to have to remind herself over and over again not to let him get under her skin. The thing was, he reminded her of Kyle…and no one had ever reminded her of Kyle before.

He just had a little bit of a harder edge to him to get to know him. But lately, that teasing and cajoling was a lot like Kyle. As if he knew how to get to her. And that meant she was going to have to watch her heart that much more carefully.

CHAPTER ELEVEN

Standing in the middle of rows and rows of grapes, Todd stared at Ginny. "Okay, halt. Let's agree to disagree on pruning—are you good with that? Because obviously it's very complicated and there are a few different ways to do it. I tend to like the way I do it and you like the way you do it. But these are *my* vineyards. So my way rules."

She met his gaze with eyes that told him she was struggling to hold back. The woman had a problem with not speaking her mind. But he wasn't going to be intimidated by her.

"Look, we seem to get along with everything except about my vineyards. I didn't come to Tyler and get into your business about your vineyards."

"Well, it's a good thing because they're mine and I do things like I want to do them there."

"And good for you. If you want to cut your vines back too much and harvest too soon, that's your prerogative. I'm assuming you do them like your parents want done too?"

Her head tilted and her eyes narrowed. "I do what I want. I'm really good at what I do. The vineyard and the wine was floundering for a lot of years when I was a teenager. I love my dad but he wasn't making the right choices. He wasn't the best at overseeing the vineyard. I turned it all around. I'm the one who made our small vineyard what it is. We're small but we do well. No, we haven't won a major award; we haven't even entered a lot. But our customer base loves our wine and our vendors, especially our vendors, keep us really busy. We could grow faster but I don't have the acreage or the manpower. If I tried to grow, I'm afraid we might go in the red. But for our size, we are outstanding and growing in reputation. And when people come to see me at my vineyard, they are usually asking for my advice and listening to me. So, it's aggravating to come here and for you not to listen to me."

He laughed. "And it's the same for me. You know ours is making a huge name for itself, and yet you come here and tell me that what you know is better than what I know."

They stared at each other. He realized that he wanted to kiss her. As maddening as the woman was, he could not get her off his mind. They had been arguing and this flirting with fire thing they had going on was starting to get to him. As if reading his mind, she lifted her chin and that challenge came into her eyes.

"Why are you staring at me like that?"

"If I told you, you wouldn't like it."

"Try me."

"No, I'm pretty sure you wouldn't like it and it isn't really about the vineyards. And you're already upset enough without me upsetting you more." He looked at the grapes surrounding them. They were out in the middle of the vineyard and it was beautiful, romantic even. He loved his vineyard, but to be honest, he had never really been out here with a woman who had him spitting mad and feeling romantic at the same time. Nope, no one got to him like his wife did.

His wife.

Wow, he was still getting used to that. He turned and walked away, needing to put some distance between them. Trying to get his thoughts back to where they needed to be and not on this arguing. The arguing only seemed to make these feelings worse.

Grapes. He needed to focus on grapes. *Or jelly.*

"Maybe we should go look at the jelly."

She had stormed up to stand in front of him and fisted her hands on her hips. "No, not jelly. You love jelly but we were talking about these grapes that you make wine with and then you're saying something was going to upset me. Don't tell me that you're going to trim this entire field back—" Her words died when he took a step toward her.

"What?" she stuttered.

105

"I was thinking that I wanted to kiss you."

She swallowed hard. Her eyes widened but she held her ground and lifted her chin at that challenge. "W-why would you be thinking that?"

He took another step toward her. They were toe-to-toe. "Because I have a problem, Ginny McCoy. When you get to being feisty like that and all determined, and argue like that, I like it." Her mouth fell open and he grinned; he couldn't help it. Seconds ticked by. He had actually made Ginny speechless.

She swallowed hard again and he watched her throat move. With a steady, deliberate movement, he reached out, wrapped his arm around her waist and tugged her to him. She came without hesitation; her chin lifted a little more and she looked straight up at him. "You are beautiful," he murmured. His pulse quickened. He knew he was making a big mistake.

And then her arms went around his neck and his arms pulled her close as their lips met.

Ginny was in so much trouble. But, at the moment, her

brain was not listening to her. It was not thinking rational; all she was thinking about was being in this man's arms, with his lips finally on hers again. Since the day they had married and he had kissed her at the ceremony, a part of her had wanted this.

Her emotions had been haywire. Her memories had flooded back. Not since Kyle had her heart been moved like this…only she wasn't thinking of Kyle right now. It was Todd.

Her husband…the man she was married to. Her heart stumbled as reality set in…the man who in less than three months she would be divorced from. Three months and she would be back in Tyler, rescuing her vineyard, working it just like she always had wanted, with no man to argue with her. No man to get in her way.

He pulled back and rested his forehead against hers. Both of them breathed unsteadily.

"What are we doing?" he asked.

"I'm not sure. I'm confused. We don't need this."

He let out a sigh. His warm breath feathered over her, sending a thrill through her.

"I know, I've been telling myself that for the past two weeks. For the past month. I've been telling myself that ever since I kissed you at the ceremony and put a ring on your finger."

"This is a business deal," she murmured.

"Right," he said, still holding her.

She knew this was a mistake, so why did it feel so right? She could get hurt.

When was the last time she had risked being hurt?

The question made her uncomfortable. And then, as if to defy that she never took a risk, she ran her fingers into his hair and tugged his lips back to hers.

CHAPTER TWELVE

Todd enjoyed the kiss more than he could fathom. He enjoyed holding Ginny. He enjoyed the moments that they stood there holding each other and kissing so much that he let sanity go.

But now, he pulled back. "We need to really think about what we're doing right now," he said, letting sanity return. Everything in him screamed that they were married and that they liked each other. But that wasn't what they had agreed on.

"You're right." She stepped away from him.

He let her go.

They stared at each other and time stretched between them.

His heart drummed a beat in his chest so hard he was sure if he looked down, he'd see his shirt moving. This felt so crazy. Ever since his granddaddy had laid out these ridiculous terms in the will, everything had been out of control and irrational. He swallowed past the dryness in his throat then plunged forward with the argument that should set them back on the right path. "We are not compatible. We're attracted to each other, but that is only going to get us in trouble."

Ginny's eyes glittered dangerously as she took a step back. And he wasn't sure whether she was angry or near tears.

"You're right." She slapped a hand to her hip and he saw the look, the one that told him clearly that she was struggling.

Struggling to be rational like he was and not let the emotions and attraction drawing them together cause them to make a mistake. At least, he thought that was what she was thinking.

But who really knew *what* she was thinking.

He held her piercing gaze and forced out his next words. "We made a business deal, and I *promised* you that nothing would happen."

"Yes, you did. And I came on board because of that."

Tensions vibrated between them like the pulsing bass of a rock band.

She held her chin up a little. "We're not good for each other anyway. Yeah, we might be attracted to each other but we disagree about everything else, just like you said."

"Yeah, everything but kissing." He hadn't meant to say that out loud but he had, and his gaze dropped to her amazing lips. They trembled slightly; she bit them to hold them still and then she frowned. Instantly, he knew he should have kept his mouth shut. His gaze flew back to the vulnerable, questioning look in her eyes that he glimpsed sometimes when her guard was down. All he wanted to do was take her back into his arms and tell her that she was worth so much more than her kisses.

"That isn't true," he tried. "We have our moments

when a miracle happens and we agree on something about the vineyards."

"Good try, but you know that isn't true. And why are we talking about this? You've got your own vineyard and I've got mine to go back to so I can make my dreams come true."

"Right. We both have a plan and we need to stick to it or we are courting disaster. So, we need to step back and reevaluate what is going on here."

"Exactly." She'd wrapped her arms across her waist. "You're right. We agree on something. And this...*this* never happened. Well, it *happened,* but it's better this way. I'm not marriage material, anyway, and I know that. I just forget when...well, my brain just loses all thought when..."

When they kissed. He filled in what she was trying so hard to not say.

"I am impetuous sometimes, if that's the right word. I'm spontaneous. I'm spastic. I do things on the spur of the moment. I'm bolder than I need to be sometimes. All of the above. I'm all of that but the one thing that I know that I'm not is marriage material. So yeah, we need to forget this happened. And go back to just having a business deal."

She spun and strode away as fast as she could.

Todd watched her go, not letting himself go after her. But he found that he wanted to go. To pull her back into his arms and tell her what she was saying about herself not being marriage material was wrong. But it was the look in her eyes, the vulnerability that he saw there, that had him locked in position and he did not move.

There was a lot to Ginny that she hid from everybody. The idea hit him hard. *Why was that?*

He wanted to find out what she hid behind those expressive eyes, and buried deep in that hidden heart of hers.

But not right now. Right now, they needed distance. They needed a lot of distance for now.

"The man is driving me crazy," Ginny declared as she slammed through the kitchen door of Allie's home. She had driven over in one of Todd's trucks and had been able to get here fast enough.

Allie gaped at her.. "Welcome to my world of a few months ago. Come on, sit down. Let me get you a cup of coffee or tea or whatever you'd like. But sit down and calm down. This is your sanctuary, your safe place. Remember, that is what we discussed. You knew going into this that you and Todd were going to get on each other's nerves…that fireworks were going to explode and that you were both going to have to compromise over these three months."

"Right. Tea please," Ginny said, tersely.

Allie headed to the refrigerator. "Focus on the prize: saving your vineyard. And he will save his."

"Right."

"Now sit down, take a deep breath and relax." Allie pulled out a pitcher of golden honey-toned Texas sweet tea. She set it on the counter, took a tall clear glass and stuck it under the ice dispenser to fill it with ice, then poured the Texas brew into her glass. She carried it over and set it in front of her. "Drink up. You know how you love sweet tea."

It was true, she did drink wine. She loved a good

wine but she wasn't a big drinker; she savored her wine. But when it came to sweet tea, oh yeah, she could drink her body weight in sweet tea. And she had an energy level of a racehorse, which enabled her to actually drink or eat whatever she wanted to. And right now, she was so revved up that however many calories were in that glass of tea, it wasn't even going to matter.

She lifted the glass and took a drink. It was delicious.

Allie crossed her arms and looked thoughtful. "I know. You need a distraction. We can take the truck down to the river and walk along the banks and let the peace work its magic on you. Or we could walk down the road and you can see my baby calves. I've got a new bunch of them. Want to feed them? They'll knock you around and you'll forget all your troubles just trying to survive and not get drug around in the muck. Believe me, I know."

Ginny laughed, getting a vivid picture of that in her brain. "I don't think I want to go wrestle with a bunch of baby cows today. And I'm not in the mood for the river either. I've got enough on my mind." She yanked her hat off. "Do you know they're harvesting my grapes out there in Tyler without me? I've never missed a harvest at my winery! *And I'm missing it.* They had to hire the people to come in and take my place. Dad's overseeing it but I'm really good at picking my grapes and he had to hire more people to take my place. We are barely speaking. It's all driving me crazy. And then, on top of that, I've got Todd McCoy not helping matters." The kiss took over her thoughts and wiped everything else out.

"Todd? Hmmm, that's sounding interesting."

Ginny gave Allie a deep frown.

"Okay, well, your dad's got it all handled and you've got to think about the big picture. I'm sorry y'all are barely speaking but I'm confident that it will work out. But big picture is you're going to miss this one harvest. This year only, because it will be all yours next year. Don't forget—if you didn't marry Todd, then you would probably have no winery or vineyard at all."

Ginny rubbed her forehead. It was true. She was going crazy and thank goodness for Allie; she was always able to calm her down. Sometimes Allie needed a push from behind, and so they balanced each other out. She and Todd certainly didn't balance each other out; they aggravated each other on a Richter scale of ten and yet he completely frustrated her hormones when he was around. The good-looking, maddening, beef-cake of a guy could melt her with a grin—if she wasn't fighting giving in with all her might.

Okay, she didn't need to think about that.

She took a long, long drink then wiped her mouth and stared at her friend. "*Seventy-two days.*"

Allie laughed. "Okay, look, you cannot do a countdown every day. You'll go crazy. Seriously— think positive about this. Speaking of harvest, isn't Todd getting ready to harvest—I mean, shouldn't they be?"

Ginny cocked her head and glared at her friend. "Point of contention. No, he is not harvesting yet. And this is one of the problems. The man refuses to take my advice. I told him he was harvesting too late, that they should've been getting ready to harvest last week and it should be happening right now. He told me that he had it handled. We differ on our opinions of harvest times. He told me that."

Allie laughed. "Ginny, he is successful at what he does. It's not a one-man show over there. I mean, you've seen his setup. He knows what he's doing and you can't just go in there and tell him how to run his business."

"Why not? He's doing it wrong. I'm just trying to help him."

Allie sat down and took a deep breath. "Ginny, you're used to running your winery exactly like you want. And you're doing well—I mean, you won honorable mention last year and that was amazing on a level that you've never seen before. You have brought that winery to what it is today and you know that you're going to be hugely successful in the next few years. I mean, I've never seen anybody so passionate about something. I know your passion and you study everything about it. There's no way you're not going to be successful. But Todd's winery is already successful. You can't expect him to welcome your criticism."

She didn't say that it was more than just their differences as winemakers that was getting to her. "I just want to be taken seriously and I guess I'm not used to not being listened to. The man doesn't listen to me at all."

"Y'all barely know each other. Give him time."

They didn't really have time. "You're right. You know what the other maddening thing is? He thinks his jelly is more important than his wine. You should see the man at the jelly factory. It's like the jelly is his gold-medal winner...well, I mean it has won awards, too, but still, to waste all that land on jelly..." She shook her head.

"Have you tasted that jelly?"

She sighed. "Yes. It is delicious. I had some on a biscuit. But just because it was amazing doesn't mean that he shouldn't devote more land to his winery. He has this amazing setup and all the state-of-the-art equipment. And he has acres and acres of rolling vines. Honestly, Allie, I'm a little bit jealous of that. You know my winery will never be anything but a small boutique winery because of the lack of growth potential. And that's fine. But to have all of this and not utilize it to its maximum potential is hard for me to take."

"I can see where that would be hard for you. You are having to settle and you are a boundary-pushing gal. He's happy where he's at. Couldn't you buy more land away from the main vineyard?"

"I could after I'm on my feet and have gained more recognition. If I play my cards right, I can make a good living at it and grow later. *If* I continue to have good luck and continue to raise grapes that are less susceptible to disease."

"You'll do it. With the money that you're going to make from Todd, you can't expand some?"

"No. I mean, it's going to take everything that I make from marrying Todd to pay my mom and dad. With them retired and traveling and getting everything they really deserve—which I'm glad they will get to do…I'm just not happy about the process they went through to get it—I won't have their help, which means I'll have to hire help, which means I'll have less money to expand, even if I did find land. It's going to take awhile."

"Don't defeat yourself with all this talk. It isn't like you. You're going to do this. You're going to be a success and you're going to get back in there and win gold or at least silver at some of these competitions you are entering. It just takes one to get some better recognition and then you'll move up and make more on your wine. Right? You'll be set."

Ginny didn't want to break Allie's bubble. Allie didn't really know that much about the winery business and it wasn't that easy. However, she did have a point. If Ginny could get a little bit more recognition and get a buyer to buy her future crops, everything would be better. And she had just admitted to Allie the part about all of this that had bothered her. She was jealous of Todd McCoy's vineyards.

She was. She hadn't really admitted that until now, but goodness gracious, his vineyard was gorgeous. What would it be like to be able to walk those vineyards every day and bring chemistry and art together, creating as much wine variations as she could come up with? Just the thought had her going off on a tangent of blends and different grape varieties. It was an electrifying thought to her. Yep, she was an odd bird. But she loved it.

She realized Allie was watching her. "What?"

Allie's lips twitched. "I just like it when I can look at you and I can see your brain churning behind those big eyes of yours. It's like a runaway roller coaster."

She made a face at Allie, making her laugh.

"So, speaking of harvesting. I heard Wade say something about a harvest festival. Are y'all getting ready? Obviously, Todd's not the only one around here who waits to harvest. August must be a good month for it. Wade says I'll be able to squash them with my feet. I remember we did that when we were young at your vineyard."

Memories of good times washed over her. Her dad and mom laughing as she and Allie jumped and danced in the wine vat and got grape juice all over them. "We didn't have grapes to waste but it was fun when we did get the chance. He did mention that they're going to have a harvest festival and he's also going to have a jelly fest, all together. That's what he does every year.

So instead of being in Tyler, helping harvest my own grapes, I'm going to be stuck here, watching him have a jelly fest and a harvest festival."

"Well, aren't you going to help him?"

"He hasn't asked me." He probably figured that they would be in all-out war mode if he had asked her to help with the harvest festival. Suddenly, she wasn't exactly thrilled about not doing something. "I think I'm going to ask him why I'm not getting to help with that. I mean, I'm bored out of my mind—doesn't he realize that? I've been making the man biscuits nearly every other day but I'm about over that until I get what I want. Does he think I'm going to stick around and make him biscuits every day?" she frowned and tapped her boot on the hardwood floor. "You're right, Allie. If they're going to be doing something at the vineyard, then I'm going to help."

Allie laughed. "There's my girl. Get in there and help him. I mean, wouldn't it be better if you could find some common ground? Ginny, have you thought that maybe you could learn something from him?"

Ginny cocked her head and her jaw stiffened as

she stared, unbelieving, at her friend. "Like what? How to make jelly? I don't have the grapes for jelly. And if he would wipe out that jelly and plant some of those better vines there, he could have a whole other wine variation to sell."

"Ginny, he likes the jelly business and it sells everywhere. Part of their empire is built off the jelly. Just because you are a wine snob doesn't mean jelly is not important."

"Right."

"Maybe you need to experiment with some jelly recipes. As much as you like to experiment."

"Nope. If I'm going to play with something, it's going to be with wine. He can play with the jelly—I'm a winemaker."

"Ginny, be open-minded. Stay calm and offer to help him with the harvest festival. We're going to come out there and enjoy the day. I'd rather see you smiling and not a stiff, angry-looking wild woman. Be nice."

Ginny sighed. "I'm not promising anything but I will at least try."

All the way back to the vineyard, she told herself to relax. To calm down. Staying all tense and aggravated would not be the way to spend the rest of her time here. And Allie was right; maybe she could learn something from him. She had to think outside the box. Who knew what she could do? She wasn't going to tell Todd this but she would be watching and maybe she could learn something.

CHAPTER THIRTEEN

Todd was in the oversized barn area that they used for the harvest festival every year. With his head overseer gone, he was having trouble keeping everything in control. Not that he would have mentioned that to anyone. But he had a lot on his plate, and right smack in the middle of all this, he had to deal with his granddaddy's plans to keep the vineyard. And then there was spending time with Ginny. *Stubborn woman. Why hadn't he asked her to help with this?*

Probably because he didn't want her taking over. But honestly, right now, that would be great. Even if they butted heads some.

"Hey." She stepped around the corner of the building. As if she had been listening to his thoughts, waiting for the right moment to jump out and startle him.

"Hey yourself," he said, remembering the last time they'd been together, kissing. He forced the memory away and watched her look around at the chaos going on around him.

There was a crew stringing lights and a crew setting up the stomping barrels. But they were all running behind. The harvest festival would happen the following weekend so they only had not quite two weeks and they had a lot to do before that time. He should have called in more recruits. He should have called in everyone he could think of, including Allie and Wade. They'd have brought some of the cowboys from the ranch, and still could if he got desperate. He should have called his cousin Caroline; she would have helped. But she was out of the country for the last few weeks. He should have asked Ginny.

Now, watching her approach, his brain went back

to kissing. He had to get his brain back on track. She was here; he needed to ask her for her help now.

Maybe they could call a truce. *And no kissing allowed.*

"I just came from Allie's and she told me about the festival." Ginny stopped to stare at him and he realized she had something on her mind. "She said that I should have offered to help you with your harvest festival. I told her you hadn't mentioned it to me, much less asked for my help. Besides, I told her we would kill each other. But she said maybe we should try to work together, or something to that effect."

She looked slightly uncomfortable. Her hot-pink cowboy hat sat low on her head and her eyes were partly shadowed. *She was so stinkin' cute.* He told himself not to think about that.

"Us—work together? Yeah, my first thought is we would probably hurt each other."

"So, we agree. Is that why you've kept this a secret?"

"No. Yeah. If I'm being completely honest, that is part of it."

"Look, back home, I would be working my butt off, getting the harvest in. Plus dealing with the everyday issues of running a winery, which you are familiar with since you not only do that, but run the jelly farm too. And since you told me you lost your head overseer, and since I never had one, I'm pretty sure I would be semi capable of doing whatever needs to be done here. I do nearly all the roles on my own back home. Although I understand your winery is much bigger than my winery—we're not here to discuss who's got the bigger one. We're here to discuss how to get this event off and running on time." She glanced around then pinned him with accusing eyes. "Because you *are* behind, right?"

Dang woman. "Yeah, you might say that. I didn't quite realize what all it took to get this thing going. And I have had my mind on other things—partly saving the vineyard by finding a wife and getting married. And then thinking about a few distracting things I had going on in my life after I married you." His gaze swept over her face and her lips, and he wanted to kick himself. "So yeah, I'm behind. And

Allie might be right on the fact that if you could possibly try to get along with me for more than a few minutes at a time, we might be able to work together and solve my problem."

"Me get along with you? How about *you* getting along with *me*?"

They glared at each other.

She hitched her chin and narrowed her eyes. "This isn't all just me, you know."

The woman could drive a saint over a cliff. Or to drink. "Where's that truce we were going to do? Okay, yes, I need to get along with you. Look, could you help me? I'm out of options. I could hire some more people but the truth is, I need somebody who kind of knows what in the heck is going on."

She grinned, rubbing it in. "Well, to be honest, I don't exactly know what is going on since I've never actually held a festival. But, I'm a very fast learner. I've looked some up online and know what goes on. The only grape stomping I've done was when me and Allie were little, my dad would let us stomp the grapes not worth using in the wine. I can handle it, though, for the festival. And then there's the putting the footprints on the T-shirts. Do you have the T-shirts?"

"They're supposed to be coming but I don't know if they'll make it in time."

"Let's just hope they do."

"Does this mean you're on board to help?"

"I am. If you promise that if I help, you'll let me go into your winery and play around a little bit."

"What do you mean 'play around'?"

"Testing. I love finding that taste, that blend that's just perfect and I want to do some testing. I've told you that. I've never had a variety like you have to work with. It's driving me crazy."

"Sure. I don't mind if you do that. I meant to take you already. It might be kind of fun to watch you. I test, but I've always let the master winemaker come up with our wines. Although he took a job in Italy just recently so I'm trying to hire a new one."

"Let me know if I can help choose one. My vineyard is small so I don't get to do a lot of experimental testing. I have my specialty, but if I had more grapes and more variety, it would be amazing what I could come up with. You might even want to hire me for your master winemaker."

He studied her, how her face lit up and how her eyes were all almost dreamy-eyed as she thought about getting in a room with a whole bunch of different varieties of grapes. Made him want to get in there with her and see what she could do. "Come on, let's do this and then let's make some wine. Only, I get to watch you and your chemistry at work."

She laughed. "Not a lot of chemistry on my end, just a lot of blending and tasting."

"I'm still in."

"Okay, then you're on. Let's get this party started. And we'll see what we can come up with. Now, you tell me what you normally do besides the stomping of the grapes. I did look at your website and it looks like you have a dinner and some tasting. Do you have some live music—did I see that?"

"Yes, we have live music. We have two different sittings: we have the morning and the afternoon, or they can come in the evening. The evening is for either group—they can come back and enjoy the evening with the live music and buy whatever they want."

"Well, it all sounds great, so we'll start with all that. And maybe, later on, we can add to it. Anyway, let's get this going, then we can talk some more about it."

"You're on."

CHAPTER FOURTEEN

Ginny stared about the large barn area that had a lot of people rushing around, bringing tables and chairs in. But they were just setting things down; there was no organization. Wine barrels cut in half and large buckets were everywhere. She assumed these would be for the grape stomping. Ginny stared at everything and then looked at Todd. "So how do you want it set up? Do you want the tables set in rows, connected or disconnected, or how's it been done in the past?"

He looked blank. "I'm here every year but I don't normally deal with this part of it. I think they're like in long rows connected. There would be several different rows with them connected. What do you think?"

"Oh, well, that's a good idea. If they went lengthwise, the stomping of the grapes is held at one end of the building and then maybe an area at the other end of the building where tables are set up with baskets of goodies for a silent auction." She envisioned people putting their bids on the baskets—she'd have to figure out what was in the baskets. And figure out what good cause the money would help. "I like the idea of people being able to spend their money on something that benefits something other than the winery. Something that helps the community. I can work with that—I can figure that out. So why don't we start lining these tables up? Get your people bringing them in to set them up where we want them rather than them over there in a bunch."

"Sounds good." He headed toward the men; she watched him talking and using his hands to describe what he wanted done. Then he came back toward her and butterflies stirred in her chest.

"Is that what you're thinking?" he asked when he

reached her.

She watched the men lining up the tables. "Exactly."

And so they both put aside their differences as they worked to get the inside of the building set up. She grabbed one end of the table and Todd grabbed the other and they carried it to where the first line-up would be.

Her thoughts were going over the different things they could do for the festival to draw more people. Todd told her that ticket sales were down just a little bit and wasn't sure why. But she assumed it was because the people selling his tickets hadn't gone out and done the job they should have. But she didn't say that. She didn't want to start out on a sour note. Allie had drilled that into her before she left to come over here and offer her help. She was determined to try to help the guy; after all, he had been her miracle. And if he hadn't had this dilemma for himself, she wouldn't have gotten this opportunity and come this time next year, she wouldn't have a vineyard to call her own. So, as much as she disliked the idea of keeping her mouth shut and getting along with Todd, she was going to. Because the worst thing they could do was to continue arguing and it not work out. Then again, they didn't argue all the time. That was part of the problem—she was just going to have to get comfortable with being attracted to the man. Because she was.

And as they worked together, she fought hard not to think about putting aside her hang-ups and getting to know the man better. But she didn't get to know anybody better. She had to remind herself that she needed to keep her distance, because if she gave in to this desire to let her guard down with him, she could run into problems.

But by the end of the evening, when the tables were actually all set up and all the help had gone for the evening, she stood there, tired but satisfied that they had accomplished so much in the third of the day that they had been working. She realized they had gotten along the whole time simply because she had kept her mouth shut and he had kept his shut except on questions about what was the best way to set up for the harvest festival.

"These baskets—I'm envisioning they include your jellies and some specialty items that we can find that have to do with Texas and maybe some of the other businesses. Have you ever thought about doing other things you could sell? You know, gift items or things that complement jelly or wine? Like cheese trays or other specialty items." It got her to thinking about her winery and all the specialty things she could offer. Things that didn't take up a lot of space but complemented her business. She didn't have the space for more vines but she could have the space for other projects. She hated to say it, but the more she was thinking about it, the more she thought that his having both the jelly and the winery might be a very smart move.

She wondered whether she could start her own jelly line, but wasn't ready to concede to him that she was thinking this. For the jelly, she could buy grapes from other vineyards. She liked testing; maybe she could come up with some unique jellies. She had seen some jalapeño jelly—there were all different kinds she could come up with. And the idea had her smiling.

"I think that not only would I like to go work in the vineyards testing room but I was thinking about maybe testing a few other recipe ideas in the kitchen."

He stared at her. "Whatever you want. I'm easy. I mean, we can't come up with something great unless you're testing, so test away."

She smiled at him and felt warmed by the genuine look of interest in his eyes. "All right, don't mind if I do. Thank you."

It had been a busy few days as Ginny dove into helping Todd one hundred percent. She was determined this was going to be the best harvest festival McCoy Wines had ever hosted. They sent out social media flyers everywhere; she called in the social media company she used for her winery to help get the word out while also working with a local marketing company Todd used. By doubling their efforts, they anticipated a large turnout. She doubled the tables and doubled the number of guides giving tours of the winery, the jelly facility, or both.

There was only two days to go until the day of the festival, she stood in the parking area, gazing at the huge banner she'd ordered and feeling good about what they'd accomplished.

"Wow, that looks great," Todd said.

She spun to find him standing behind her, hands on his lean hips, his cowboy hat knocked back a bit, and squinting at the sun. The man looked good no matter what, even rumpled and with stubble on his face. Her breath caught and she told herself to get a grip.

"Don't you love it? I was pleased when it arrived just a little bit ago. Do you like the way your logo looks with the vineyard photo behind it? I like the aspect of giving both your businesses equal time."

His smile widened. "Do you now?"

She smiled, glad that he didn't totally dismiss her idea and a little bit thrilled that he acted as if he actually liked it.

"Speaking of harvesting, how's harvesting going at your place?"

She had spoken to her dad earlier that morning,

despite things being tense between them she'd called to ask about the harvest. "Dad assures me that it's going well. Honestly, I'm not sure how to take that. I guess I don't want to admit that my winery can work fine without me."

"I have a feeling that that's not completely true. I have this gut feeling that the energy that you bring to your winery is a big part of its charm. If I'm correct in my assumption, I'd say that you are the biggest draw to your winery. You probably define your winery. I must confess that I tasted your wine the other day, and it's excellent. It's got a spark to it and an energy, which is just like you. There are no mellow, gentle tones—it's bold and impressive."

She was speechless. She stared at him, dumbfounded. "You like my wine?" she asked at last.

"Yeah. Is that hard to believe?"

"No. I love my wine. I guess I just thought that with your wine and the ease with which you've gotten accolades and haven't even completely focused on winemaking, I assumed my wine wouldn't be something you would really care for."

"You assume too much."

She laughed. "Maybe so. Okay, so let's get on with this. We've got the jelly area set up. We're going to offer tastings. I talked to Clara and Ethel and they are going to oversee this section. I guess they've done it before and they are on board. I told them to pull out everything. And we're going to have some coloring booths for the kids over there and because you know they are probably your number-one demographic, we are going to do a lot of things to make the day special for them. We're going to have some fun grape races and we're going to have them do some grape stomping too, but it's not going to pertain to the wine, but rather the jelly. I think it will be a lot of fun. We're still coming up with exactly what, but we will have it figured out by tomorrow. And then over to the wine area. I'd like to go over what we're offering in the tour. Do you have a moment or have thirty minutes to run and take a look?"

"I'm all yours."

That had her brain going completely to other subjects that had nothing to do with grapes, wine, or jelly—and everything to do with him and her. "Okay then, let's go. I've got the buggy over here." They walked over to the ATV and climbed in. "Hang on, cowboy. I like driving these things."

He laughed and grabbed hold and she took off.

CHAPTER FIFTEEN

Todd laughed as Ginny sped down the gravel drive that connected the vineyards to the vat rooms, which was a huge red barn that housed all the barrels and the vats. It was a good distance through the vines from the actual house and she laughed as she pressed the gas pedal of the little open-aired vehicle and they tore across the land.

"You weren't kidding when you said you liked to drive these things."

She grinned at him as the wind blew her hair and her eyes sparkled with vibrancy. He was mesmerized by her. And she was putting her all into this.

"No, I wasn't kidding. These things are meant to be driven. I like to take them off-road, too, but of course, I don't see any off-road trails here so these gravel roads will have to do. I like to feel the wind in my hair."

"Well, it's in there and in mine, too, and my hair is nowhere near as long as yours."

She did a little zigzag with the ATV and he had to grab his hat. "Hey now, you make a man lose his cowboy hat and you're in for trouble."

"I didn't lose mine." She cackled.

Today she had on a lime-green hat that looked as though someone had beaten it with a baseball bat and then pinned a bright-red jewel to the front of it. "And may I say that your cowboy hat is really lovely."

She was paying attention to the road but she grinned wide, making him laugh. "Hey, don't be making fun of my cowboy hat. Just because I like to stomp on it a little bit. Make it look worn—have a little character. A little different from the pristine perfect hat that you wear."

"Nothing wrong with a cowboy hat looking good. Every cowboy I know wants their cowboy hat to look good."

"And I agree. I like your hat. But I like mine beat up and this one in particular is my lucky hat. I've had this hat the longest of any that I've owned. I got it when I was fifteen and I've been buying them ever since."

"So that's why it looks the way it does. It's what, ten years old?"

"Something like that."

So that made her twenty-four or five. She was about the age he suspected but when he met her he thought she was just a smart aleck. Now he realized she was still a smart aleck but she knew what she was talking about. It had just taken him awhile to realize that. He had really been impressed with her wine. It was different than anything he had ever tasted. And now that he looked at her, he wanted to make sure she understood exactly what he meant.

She pulled the ATV up in front of the building.

"Yeah, I'm actually startled that you know so

much. You impress me."

She tilted her head and just stared at him as if she couldn't believe he'd said such a thing. "I started studying vines and how to grow the grapes early. And when I was old enough, I started experimenting with wine combinations. I love creating. You can actually get the different bottles through the years and see my development. My dad had completely given over the creating to me over the last few years. I've been working so hard, trying to take it to another level, refining the Rossi Rose of Tyler wine flavor, and depth and complexity. My hope is that in the next five years, I can achieve my bigger dreams."

"Well, I can tell you that honestly just in the last few days, when we've been talking and I've been watching you work so hard, I can see you achieving anything you set your mind to."

A look of pleasure came across her face and he liked that gleam in her eye. He could tell that she was very proud of the knowledge she had and he kind of felt bad that he had dismissed her knowledge early on. "I really am sorry about misjudging you."

"I misjudged you too."

They stared at each other and he had that crazy desire to pull her into his arms and kiss her again. He was starting to have that thought more and more. He wasn't sure it was a good thing to be wanting, considering she was determined to go back to her home and her vineyard. She had no desire to stick around at the end of the three-month period.

CHAPTER SIXTEEN

The entire time they were touring and going over the specifics about the things she wanted done in the vat room as people came through, including small tastings, he was distracted by everything because he was watching her.

Ginny came alive when she was discussing anything that had to do with the wine industry but especially creating the wine. Her eyes sparkled and as she discussed it with his foreman, he crossed his arms and just listened. When Jacob would look at him to see whether what she was wanting was okay with Todd,

Todd would nod. Her ideas were good and he wasn't going to mess up her good humor by changing anything. This wasn't his cup of tea, anyway; that's the reason he had had his foreman over all this. He was glad to have her input and once he saw how excited she was about all of it, he was too. When they had left and got outside after, she had pointed out that the entrance needed a lot of flowers. She wanted wine barrels brought in, full of flowers; she wanted them overflowing with geraniums and periwinkles and marigolds. With only the last of the day and tomorrow to get it done, he wasn't sure it could happen.

"We'll need to make a run to Fredericksburg's Wild Seed Farm and grab what you need."

"Can I go with you? I haven't been there and I hear it's gorgeous. Just fields and fields of flowers."

"Sure. Let's go now because we're running out of time."

"Didn't I see a small nursery right there in Stonewall? I bet to save time we could find what we need there."

"Right, let's do that. I'd like to give locals as

much of an opportunity to be seen as possible."

"Sounds like a plan." She looked around and sighed, squinting into the sunshine and looking happier than he had seen her looking since she arrived.

He liked it. "What are you thinking?"

"That I agree—I think we're almost ready and I really like your vineyard, Todd. It's beautiful and well thought out. And you produce wonderful wine. I did a few small tastings myself."

"Well, I think we are mutual admirers of each other's wine. Now let's go find these flowers so we can spruce up the outside of this place. I think you're right; we might need flowers in a whole lot of other places. Should I take a trailer?"

"I don't know. How much are we thinking? I mean, there's going to be ample room for more flowers in various sections of the event. We can have barrels of flowers near the wine stomping and at the entrance area of the grape tasting festival area. You have beautiful flowers at the villa. You obviously have someone who takes care of those."

He gave a rueful laugh. "I do. Honestly, the Flower Spot came out and landscaped after we had a big freeze that froze everything. Now my own groundskeeper takes care of them. I have to be honest, I just walk out and see them. Too many other things on my mind to deal with the flowers."

"And thus the reason why you don't have them all over the place. When I go back to Tyler, you'll have to come and see my little place. We have roses everywhere, because Tyler's kind of famous for their rose emporium and all the different variations of roses they have. I almost have as many flowers as I do grapes, my dad always teases me."

"And do you plant and take care of all these flowers?"

"Some of them but they're pretty maintenance-free—just takes a little watering and irrigation. And if there's one thing a vineyard has, it's irrigation."

True. He smiled at her then they climbed into the ATV and raced back to the truck. He drove to town with much more care than she drove.

Ginny liked Todd. *How many times did she have to say to herself that she was in deep trouble?* But she did like him a lot. And they surprisingly worked well together; of course, he had said yes to everything she wanted, so she delighted in that fact. And it made her admit that sometimes maybe she needed to give a little instead of just taking from this relationship that they had for the time being. As they drove down the curvy road back toward Stonewall, they talked about his growing up with his granddad. Because she was curious about the man who had left such an odd will for his boys.

"So y'all had no clue that when he died he was going to give you these odd requirements? I mean, I can relate in a way because I had no idea my dad was going to sell mine out from under me. Sometimes you just wonder about these main men in our lives—your granddad and my dad. Not to be disrespectful—I love my dad dearly and I know you loved your granddad. And I know that my dad loves me and I know that your granddad loved you and your two brothers. But I don't know...this is just so strange on both of their parts."

"We had zero idea that he was going to do this. But we've decided—and Allie helped us with this too—he really wanted great-grandchildren, enough to force us to marry. And us being adult men, we've been building our careers and finding our own way and not having a big influence of a female anymore since our mom was not here. We just hadn't been paying attention to how much he wanted great-grandkids. I guess he just went to drastic measures. But this isn't the way it should have been done."

He pulled into the driveway of the Flower Spot. He kept the engine on and turned to look at her. "Forcing us to get married—it is just wrong on all sorts of levels. And I have to admit that I was totally surprised that Allie and Wade were able to make it work."

She was not delusional enough to think that in any way, shape, or form that the two of them would ever be an actual couple. And why would she even be entertaining that thought in the first place? But right now, looking at him, she was entertaining the thought of kissing him again.

"I think that everything aligned just perfect for Allie and your brother. No, I don't think that it's going to be a normal thing and while I will admit that you are far more charming than I originally thought—and don't get a big head just because I said that—I do like your winery. But I am not Allie. I will probably never marry for real. It will be me and a bunch of cats and dogs at my vineyard. I'll be puttering around there when I'm a hundred, tending to my vines." She laughed, seeing the picture.

"I could see you being a hundred and still puttering around but I don't see you single the rest of your life. Why would you say that?"

Like a lightning bolt, a strike of pain sliced through her as she thought of Kyle.

"I have my reasons."

"I hate to admit that I'm very curious about them."

She was surprisingly tempted to spill her guts to this man. *Why was that?* "We better get in there and look at those flowers before they start to wonder why this big truck is sitting out here." She opened the door and climbed out. Hopefully ending the conversation.

Todd met her at the front of the truck. "I'm going to hound you about this, you know. You are my wife, after all, and I'm curious to know why you think you're going to be single."

His eyes were serious and she got the impression that he wasn't kidding about hounding her.

The question was, was she going to tell him?

After they'd chosen all the flowers she wanted, Todd and Ginny climbed into the truck and headed back. They rode in silence but his thoughts were churning. And he figured hers were, too, as she watched the land pass by. Several times he thought about saying something but all he wanted to ask her again was why. He was kind of obsessed with it by the time they pulled into the driveway and he turned off the engine.

She hopped from the truck without saying anything.

He followed her. He touched her arm. "Ginny, why? I've been quiet but I can't figure out why you plan on never marrying for real. I'm curious. As angry as you are at your parents, you need to let it go. They are trying to act out of love and for some reason, they thought that you'd be better off starting over than having the winery hanging around your neck and weighing you down. Don't you think that they thought they were giving you a new chance?"

She spun toward him, her face contorted with more anger than he had seen since they had been together—even more anger than he had seen toward him. "Todd, they were giving away—selling—my birthright, basically. The only place I've ever known...the only place I've loved and they didn't ask me. It's hard to forgive something like that."

"Yes, but have you ever thought that there might be more to the story and they're trying to do this for you? They're giving you this shot now. Luckily, my grandfather and my weird will all worked out well. I would have found something, even if you didn't come along. I would have found a way to save it. I'm not letting it go. Never."

"And as far as why I'm going to stay single the rest of my life...it's because when you give your heart to someone, you open up yourself to all kinds of pain. And to be quite frank, Todd, I've been through that once, a long time ago. And it nearly killed me."

They stood close; she glared up at him, her face full of pain, anger, and anguish. The mesh of emotions tore at him. Not able to stop himself, he placed a hand along her jawline and cupped it gently. He stroked her cheek. "I didn't know. I'm so sorry you've been hurt like that. And I had no idea." She'd been hurt and he ached for her. There was pain in her eyes. He wanted to comfort her and protect her. And this was not the time or place for that. "If you ever need to talk, I'm here. And Ginny, seriously, I support you but you need to let it go with your mom and dad. You might not always have them. They won't be here forever and I can tell you from my own experience if something happens to them and you have unresolved issues, it will plague you for the rest of your life. Let it go— make amends." He let his hand drop away. It took an effort but then he backed up a step.

She stared at him. "You speak like you have some background in that?"

He pulled a load of flowers from the back and shot her a look. "Oh yeah, I do. And I can tell you, you don't want to carry that burden with you." With that, he turned and carried the flowers into the barn.

She trailed him. "I'm sorry about your mom and dad. I can see that you're hurt about it—it's painful. Were y'all fighting or something before they died?"

"Yeah, you could say that. Dad wouldn't let me help enough, wouldn't give me free rein. When they left the house to go to the airport, I was up in my room and wouldn't come out. Didn't tell them bye, didn't tell them I was sorry for yelling at them the day before. I just sat up there and stewed. And I never saw them again. Never talked to them again. And I've lived with that all my life." He turned and found Ginny right beside him. To his surprise, she wrapped her arms around him and laid her head on his chest.

"I'm so sorry. So sorry. I know from experience that when you lose someone, you always want one last moment with them—one last spoken word. And I can tell you it doesn't matter if you end on a good note or a bad note—the pain is there; it's always unfulfilled. But," she looked up at him, "I know in my heart that if you loved them, they know it. And all the stuff that came between you that was negative is wiped away. I just feel it in my heart that in that moment it's wiped away."

He cupped her face; he couldn't help it. "I want to believe that and that's what gets me by because I knew that they knew I loved them. That in my heart of hearts, it would have been better if I just kept my mouth shut and said 'yes, sir' to what my daddy wanted me to do. Took my time and waited for my turn. He always wanted what was best for me."

"Like my daddy always said, a good dad doesn't always get to say yes; most of the time they have to say no. But it's a process and it grows us up and makes us hard-working, loving, responsible individuals. And you are."

Her words shook a chord within him. "And you are, too, Ginny." And then, unable to stop himself, he dropped his lips to hers and kissed her.

CHAPTER SEVENTEEN

Ginny could not get enough of Todd's kiss. She wrapped her arms around him and clung to him, as if she were a starving woman. But the reality was she hadn't been kissed in so many years that she had forgotten what it was like. But something about kissing Todd was different. And she couldn't put her finger on it. It was just different. It was so searing; it filled her completely. It filled her with heat and hunger and want, and she loved it. And all he was doing was kissing her. His kiss lingered. When he pulled away to look at her, she felt as if something momentous had just happened in her life. And it scared her to death.

She backed up. "Well, I can see that we definitely have chemistry. Anyway, thanks for the sympathy and the empathy. Maybe we need to get these plants out of the truck." With that, she turned and basically strode out of the barn so fast she should have been running. In her heart of hearts, she was. Todd didn't just scare her; he wasn't just trouble—he was a threat to everything she had planned for her life and right now she totally understood it.

Todd's phone rang as he watched Ginny strut from the barn, all strong and resilient and closed up so tight that nobody was getting in, not even him. *Did he want in?* He was beginning to think he did. Did he like it? *No way.* But he couldn't shake the feeling. He had never been intrigued; he had never been put in his place; he had never been so completely enthralled by anyone. She challenged him. She riled him up. She made him want things he shouldn't be thinking about. And yet, he was.

"Hello," he said into the phone, glad for the reprieve and excuse not to follow her. This conversation didn't need to continue right now. He needed to gather his wits about him. And he had a feeling she had needed to do the same. They had been talking about too much personal stuff. That's what was wrong; they had crossed over that line that they didn't need to cross over. "Wade, is that you?"

"Yeah, it's me. Can you get over here to the ranch? I've got a problem down here with some cows and I need extra hands. You got time?"

"Oh yeah, I've got time. We got this pretty much in the bag here at the vineyard. I'll be there in a minute."

"Allie's coming to take your place if you need her to, so we will just flip-flop."

He suddenly thought that would be a great idea. "Allie has time?"

"Yup, she does. She's been wanting to come over there anyway but I wouldn't let her. Sorry, I was trying to let you guys have some time together."

"Brother, don't be getting into my personal life.

Send her over. Nothing's happening here."

He had just lied to his brother. There was plenty happening here but he wasn't going to admit it to anybody.

Ginny had started repotting plants after Todd left. She'd needed something to take her frustrations out on. *Todd*...the man just caused all kinds of craziness going on inside her. They had both butted into each other's problems; they had gotten too close. She had meddled in his life and he had meddled in her life and they didn't need to do that. When he had stormed out of the barn and told her that he had to go help Wade at the ranch with something and that Allie was coming over to help, she had been so relieved. She needed to talk to Allie.

Thirty minutes later, when Allie had gotten out of the truck and headed toward her, she had a smile on her face. But as she got closer, her smile faded. "Are you okay? You look...mad? Upset? Something. Talk to me, girl."

Ginny rocked back on her heels and placed her elbows on her knees, her hands still holding a geranium, and looked at Allie. "Allie, you know I don't get personal with people. You are about the only one—well, the only one. But for some reason, Todd pulls things out of me sometimes and it makes me nervous."

Allie's expression softened. She picked up a flower and knelt beside her. "Ginny, it doesn't hurt to let somebody else in. Tell me, do you have feelings for Todd? Because I don't think you would open up to him if there wasn't something inside you that was pulling you   toward   him." She and Allie were like twins. They had shared their lives together and Allie had always been her steady point. She was now, too. Allie calmed her in a way nobody else could, made her wish she could be different from this bull in a china closet she was most of the time. There was a goodness in Allie that Ginny just didn't feel like she had. When she was with Allie, Allie made her think that she could anyway. "I might. But Allie, it scared me to death. And there's no reason for me to admit it anyway, because I'm going to go back to my winery and I told him I was going to stay single for the rest of my life. You know, like I told you I always would after...well, you know, after Kyle."

"And like I've always told you, that's nonsense. There's a man out there for you who's going to be perfect. He's going to want a strong, independent woman like you. He's going to love your ideas. He's going to love your fire and, to be honest, the moment I saw you and Todd shooting fireworks off at each other basically that first time, I just had this gut feeling that he was the one. And then this craziness happened with what your mom and dad were doing and well, I'm just wondering if it could be meant to be. I know Wade and I were meant to be—there's no other way to put it. What happened to us couldn't just happen to anyone. What do you think?"

"I think what happened to you and Wade was a one-in-a-million shot. Couldn't happen again. I think you've got your hopes wound up for no reason."

CHAPTER EIGHTEEN

"I don't see why you think I have my hopes up." Allie dug out a hole and placed the geranium into it, covering it up and patting the dirt nice and firm. "I'm not hoping. I'm wanting…yeah, I guess I'm hoping. I don't know, Ginny. It just drives me crazy every time you say something like you're going to grow old by yourself. Honey, I know that you loved Kyle. And I know that he went away and that he died—it's just horrible. And then your dad and your mom and everybody in town just assumed all kinds of things about you that were wrong and none of their business. But you need to get over all that. It's been so long ago. Surely you're not going to let that hang over your head the rest of your life. Come on, look at me and tell me you're going to give this thing with Todd a shot."

Ginny stared at her friend, exasperation just pulling her in every direction. Everything Allie said was true. Why had she let it hold her back for so long? She was so bad about holding grudges like that—or was it even a grudge? It was just the way she felt. "Allie, I can't even tell you if there for sure is anything between Todd and me. He kissed me and kind of turned my world upside down there for a little while. And I would be lying if I said that I didn't like it and that I wasn't hoping for another kiss. I kind of do but it wouldn't work. My dream's in Tyler. I want to build my winery. I want to watch it be the best small winery there is. I want to perfect it and my label. I, just, well, I like it here. I think it's beautiful but my heart is in Tyler. Yeah, I'm really jealous of this place. I could only imagine if I had all this to work with. It would be amazing. I think right after the festival, we're going to go and I'm going to get to test a lot of their stuff and just play. I think that's what I'm going to do for the rest of the time that I'm here—I'm going to go in there and I'm going to see what I can come up with. It will help me know if there's another grape that I can grow at my place to get the blends that I want. It would be down the road. Or I'm kind of hoping that I can maybe, if I come up with something that I really like, then I could contract so many pounds of the grapes and get the taste joined with my grapes for that new blend. Anyway, I have high hopes and well, you know how I am about that stuff."

Allie smiled. "Oh yeah. I know how you are. Your brain is working and I don't think Todd realizes that when you get up in that room with all that wine and those test tubes and samples, you're just going to zone out and completely be ignorant of anyone and everybody around you."

Ginny thought about it; a smile tugged her lips and then bloomed big. "It's going to be pure bliss, is what it's going to be. I can't wait and well, the guy thinks—at least now—that I do know what I'm talking about.

And I know that he also does. He has a natural ability and I think the digging in the dirt part is the part he likes the most. But creating the wine—that's not his big deal. His wine master left and he's just kind of been floundering a little bit, I think. But his head overseer went, too, so he's been in a little bit of a bind and I don't think he realizes it. You know, you always have a reserve back there, I guess, and this place is big enough to have that. But if he doesn't get busy with this harvest…well, I just feel like he's going to miss out on a good year."

"Well, maybe while you're in there, in that room, holed up with all his wine, you can come up with a blend to tweak his too."

Ginny thought about that. "Who knows? Who knows?"

Allie looked at her, a funny look in her eyes. "You're right, Ginny. Who knows—this could end up being a match made in heaven. I mean, he's missing the key ingredients to making his winery have the taste and the blends, and here you are—that's where your joy comes from and where you excel. You just haven't had a shot at the big leagues. I know you love your winery but it's small potatoes compared to this. You're over here in the big leagues, honey. Why don't you see what you can do? I'm seeing in my mind what could happen if you two teamed up. I mean, really, it's like what you were saying about you using your vines and his vines together—it could be really cool."

Ginny grabbed the flat of flowers and moved to the other wine barrel.

Allie followed her. Allie didn't kneel back down; this time she stood there with her hands on her hips. "You're thinking about it, aren't you? I mean, you really are, aren't you?"

Ginny laughed. "Okay, okay, yes, smart aleck. I'm thinking about it. But don't hold me to that. And don't think anything's coming of this. I'm just going to keep an open mind about it. That's a huge difference from anything personal lasting between us. Remember, this is still business. Strictly business."

But even as she said the words, she knew that she was lying to herself because this had already gone way past business. This was probably already as personal as anything in her life had ever been since Kyle.

Todd's expression was grim as he stared at the dead bull that Wade had called him to come look at. "What did that?"

"I'm not liking what my first guess is and that's why I called you." Wade stood beside him, staring at the gruesome carcass. It lay out in the middle of the pasture, not too far from the house, and the whole side of its face had been ripped off and was gone. The wound was nice and neat. You could see there had been a little bit of a struggle and there was a little bit of torn up grass, but other than that it was a fairly neat kill site.

Todd's thoughts were going exactly where his brother's were. "Is that a paw print?" He strode over and looked down at the imprint in the dirt. It was definitely a paw print. A very large paw print.

"Yup, it's a paw print. You know, over time we've had reports of cougars out here but they're just so rare. I don't know the last time I heard someone reporting something killing one of their cows, though." Wade studied the landscape to make sure the big cat was gone.

There had been reports all over Texas off and on of people killing a mountain lion or panther; some called them a chupacabra. By whatever name it was called, it wasn't something a rancher wanted hanging around. Especially if it could take down a bull like this.

Todd didn't like this. "Did you call the game warden?"

"He's on his way. They'll come and they'll be able to tell us what they think. You and I both know it was a cat. My only thing is, if it decided to take down a bull, do you think it's hungry or you think maybe something's wrong with it? I mean, I'm not liking this at all. They move in a really big range. I haven't said anything about this to Allie."

"Yeah, I don't think that's a real good idea. But I wouldn't let her go wandering off by herself. If I were you, just to be on the safe side, I'd make sure all my guys have their rifles with them or a gun tied to their hip. I know I may be overreacting but I'd rather

173

overreact for a little while until we know there's nothing wrong with this cat because maybe there's just something about this bull that attracted him. I'm at a loss…I am really at a loss here. But I know I'm going to warn my people, because we're just down the road and across the highway. Who knows—he could be down there right now. Thankfully, there's a lot of things going on out here in the backcountry."

"I hear you and believe me, I'll be letting them know." He got a phone call then. From what he was saying, Todd knew it was the game warden; he was giving him directions on how to get out to the back pasture where they were. He had already given his cowboys notice to start moving the cattle out of the pasture. He didn't want to have any more missing or dead. He especially didn't want any calves to be taken.

And that was the strangest part—why would this cat take down this bull? Of all animals to take down, it was the biggest and the strongest. Why this bull instead of taking down a weaker, small calf? Unless, maybe it tried to take down something smaller and the bull got in the way. Maybe the bull was territorial.

Todd wasn't sure but he had an uneasy feeling in his gut.

The game warden came out and took samples and pictures of the tracks and the bull; they looked underneath him, looking for any other signs, and then they tracked the cat. They found a few more tracks a bit farther out. And there was no denying that it was a big cat. Wasn't a bobcat—there were plenty of bobcats around here but a bobcat couldn't do this. They were small; no way could they do this. The game warden agreed.

By the time they left, they were going to make sure to let the other ranchers in the area know to keep watch. Until they could figure out why it would take down a big bull like that, they were all going to be on alert. But the best scenario they could come up with was that, from the scuffle, it looked as if they could have an injured calf out there somewhere and that the bull had intervened. It would take more than one swipe to take him down and a cat that could do that with a paw that size—you wouldn't want to run into him without some form of protection.

By the time Todd headed home, he and Wade had both firmly decided that their women wouldn't be moving around without some sort of form of protection or without one of them with them. He realized after he was driving back to the vineyards that he had called Ginny *his woman*. And he didn't even have to talk to Wade about it. He knew just from talking to Wade the other day that he thought he had feelings for her that he wasn't accepting. Wade was already cheerleading over there for him to have the same kind of good luck with Ginny that he had had. Todd just hadn't yet decided that it would be good luck. He was going to have to grab hold of this ride and see where it went.

Because he and Ginny both had hang-ups. And nobody but the two of them could come up with help for what was next.

A few minutes later, Ginny gaped at him. "What do you mean, a cat? A mountain lion killed a bull? I've heard of some of them being spotted—last year, there were one or two up in Fort Worth and some of the busier areas of Texas. I even saw some pictures of them and they were huge. But there's so few of them. Surely, surely it's gone. There is going to be a lot of people here tomorrow."

Ginny could only think of the fact that they were about to have a festival and there were going to be a lot of people here. They had had expectations of a lot and now, after the efforts that they had been making, there were going to be people all over this place. The very idea that somebody could come to the winery and could run into a mountain lion—it was scary. That would be media exposure that they did not want.

It dawned on her, just as she was thinking that, that she responded as if this were her place too. Her brain was completely muddling things up. Todd stood with his hands on his hips, sweat dampening the V of his shirt and his armpits. They had been working; he hadn't even told her until they had finished working later in the evening what he had gone to Wade's for. There had been a lot going on with everybody finishing the last-minute details. Tomorrow, all they had to do was set things out and wait for people to show up. As they stood there, the sun started to set. It was beautiful: the cirrus clouds were spread out, and the sun was a brilliant combination of golds and the most dazzling translucent orange she had seen in a long time. It was amazing.

But she was very uneasy. "What are we going to do?"

He cocked his head so he could look at her. "We're going to be cautious and we're going to go about our business like this hasn't happened. The likelihood of him showing up here is probably about the same as you winning millions off a lottery ticket. But the fact that he showed up at Wade's and killed that bull...I'm not putting anything out of my mind. Could be deranged, you know, so I will instruct my men to have their rifles with them—not that our guests will see them but on the perimeters. We will have people watching and you'll be fine if you are here. But if you get on that vehicle and you head out anywhere, you take that pink Loretta you got with you. Do you understand? And you keep her handy, or you come and get me or one of the men who's carrying to escort you.

I don't want you going out by yourself."

"Todd McCoy, I can take care of myself. I can't believe you're telling me to keep Loretta close." She smiled. "But believe me, I'll take Loretta with me. I don't need some cowboy hanging out with me. If that cat comes at me, wanting trouble, he'll get it." His gaze hardened. "Ginny, sometimes you really do get on my last nerve. I know you're tough. I know you think you're tougher than you are. But we're talking about a cat with a paw bigger than your foot. That cat ripped the jaw off that bull with one clean swipe. You will be cautious. If you're not, I'm not giving you another warning—if I find you out here and you're roaming around and you aren't packing or if you're out there taking chances, I'll lock you in your room or I'll send you packing."

She glared at him. "Todd McCoy, again—you don't need to be giving me orders. I'll take care of myself. And if you were to try to take me and lock me in my room, then we would have a major problem."

He yanked his hat off and raked his hand through his hair. "Look, Ginny, I'm not saying this to be mean.

I'm saying this because I'm concerned about you. And you don't take well to being too concerned."

She sighed. "Okay, fine. No, I don't take well to orders. I never have. And I know that this is out of concern. So, because of that, I'm going to try to bear it. But I'm warning you—don't you try to pick me up and lock me in that room. I have Loretta in there and I'll blow that door off."

He laughed. His laugh relieved some of the tension between them and she smiled. They stared at each other. "Fine. If you're doing something that I deem is unsafe and careless and puts you at risk, then I will have a conversation with you. How does that sound?"

She shot him a grin. "Sounds like you're learning." She laughed. To be truthful about it, it felt kind of good to have someone that concerned about her. But she wasn't going to tell him. No sir, she wasn't going to tell him that.

CHAPTER NINETEEN

The day the harvest festival finally arrived, all their expectations were realized as people came in droves. Todd stood in the center of the festival area and looked at all the people milling around, enjoying the festivities. People were stomping grapes; kids were having a blast at the jelly area that had been the brainchild of Ginny. He still couldn't believe that in all the years that they had done a harvest festival, they had never incorporated something like that. With the jelly making, kids were having a blast and the parents were too.

Wade walked up to him. "I would call this a success."

Todd laughed. "You think?"

"Oh yeah. Morgan's going to be impressed. He's supposed to be flying in any minute. We're going to see that plane shooting in over there. He's going to the back pasture and I'll go pick him up. He just let me know that they were getting close. I told him to look down as they flew over this area and take a shot of it from upstairs." He laughed.

"Well, I hope the plane tilts a little bit so he can get a good shot through that window."

They heard the hum of a plane engine and looked up and saw the sleek jet flying over. His brother didn't get to come in that much but the fact that he was flying in for the festival meant one of two things: he was flying in to check in on Ginny and Todd's relationship—because Todd was sure he was starting to get a little bit nervous about what Granddaddy had planned for him. Then again, he might just be coming in to enjoy the festival. They went way back with this festival but, seriously, this was probably the best turnout they'd ever had. They hired marketing teams but Ginny went all-out about getting them to put the word out. She was really good. He wondered whether she realized that there were probably a lot of other jobs out there for her in the wine industry that had nothing to do with the vineyard. He had a feeling her mother and dad knew that too. They also knew the uncertainty of a small vineyard and the labor that was involved. He had no doubt that they had been given an opportunity of a lifetime to let this corporation come in and buy their winery and them walk away not only with their retirement intact but Ginny having a secure future. What parent wouldn't want to do that for their child? But Ginny—she was a stubborn woman and she was going to only have it the way she wanted to have it. She probably wasn't concerned about a secure future. She thought in the here and now. And she was good at it.

He might mention this to her. Try to butt his nose in where he knew he probably wasn't wanted...but maybe he could help her smooth some of this anger she was feeling at her parents—maybe he could smooth that out a little bit for her. Kind of repay her for what she had done here. He spotted her over near the grape jelly, laughing at some kids.

"You go pick up Morgan. I'm going to go over there and tell Ginny what a great job she's done." Wade grinned at him. "You do that, little brother. And while you're at it, you might try to keep her here. You two make a good team."

He wasn't even going to deny it because it was true.

Ginny spotted Todd walking toward her. She beamed at him. She was having a blast. And by the looks of him, she could tell he was happy too. This was a gigantic success. She had been hanging out with Allie, who was manning the jelly table with Ethel and Clara. And she was deciding that she liked the jelly making part of the vineyard more and more. There were aspects of it that were really fun. Like playing with all these kids.

"Hey, cowboy. What do you think?"

He grinned and tapped her cowboy hat on the front brim, knocking it down over her eyes. "I think that you did good—real good. This is the best festival ever."

She nudged her hat back up to where she could look at him. Butterflies soared inside her. The man just did something to her. She wasn't going to think about that. "Thank you. I told you I was good. All you had to do was just listen."

He pushed his head back and laughed heartily. The sound of it sent the butterflies dancing to the pit of her stomach. *She could listen to that laugh forever.* The thought slammed into her and she sobered. Just stared at him. *She could listen to that laugh and look at that man forever. Goodness gracious, she was in trouble.*

"Umm, they're fixing to start the three-legged race. And I promised those couple of boys over there and those two little girls who were fixing a team up that I'd race them. I know it would be a little bit uneven, you and me racing the kiddos, but I figured they have youth on their side. Would you want to partner up with me?" The minute the words were out, it hit her that she wouldn't mind that at all—more than just partnering in the three-legged race. She pushed that thought away. *No thinking about that.* But there was no denying that it was true.

He grinned. "I think that that sounds like a real fun idea. I'd be happy to do that."

"Great. Then get ready. We're going to go over there and get in line and find us a little string over there." She walked over and picked up one of the strips of cloth that they had supplied. She walked back over, bent down, and began tying her leg to his leg.

"Now, have you ever done a three-legged race before?" She looked up at him. He had his hands on his hips, like he did half the time, while he looked down at her. He looked like a long, tall Texan from her view. And he was so handsome it made her heart start thudding. She had to get her mind back on track.

"I have to say, it's been a very long time since I did this. I'm going to have to hang on to you and you're going to have to lead the way."

"Well now, that sounds like a mighty fine idea because you know how I am—I like to lead the way.

And I'll tell you how to do this. Because I've done it a few times."

He grinned. "Really? You go play with kids a lot and run up and down with your leg tied to somebody?"

She winked. "Maybe. There's a lot of things about me, Todd McCoy, that you don't know. I'm not just a pretty face, you know, or an amazing body. I have other things that I like to do."

"I happen to like your amazing body." The words were a reaction to her teasing about her body. He grinned. "Don't look so startled. I like you just the way you are. Especially when you're having a good time and teasing. Not that sourpuss, frowny person you are half the time." He laughed.

They grinned at each other. And then she stood and he wrapped his arm around her waist and tugged her close. She wrapped her arm around his waist and she decided they could just stand like that for as long as they wanted to.

There were more who decided to join in the race when they saw there were some adults and Todd was really happy about that because he did not feel right racing against a bunch of little kids. The kids seemed awfully excited about it. They were teasing Ginny, who had obviously made very good friends. She was teasing them right back.

"All right, you little fellas and girls. I'm going to beat you all—you better run really fast." Ginny kind of bent down, ready to run as though she were at a starting gate and they were fixing to shoot off a gun at the beginning of a race. The kids were giggling and laughing; a couple of boys, who looked to be about ten to twelve, got down like her. One of them had blond hair and the other one had brown hair and they were grinning.

"Miss Ginny, I'm going to beat you—we are. Come on, Bo, get ready."

"I am ready, Jack. You get ready."

Todd laughed. He bent down and whispered in Ginny's ear. "You're not going to beat them, are you?" She looked up at him. "Well, I am if you help me. If you don't, we're going to fall down and probably get skunked."

He grinned at her. "You really would beat those kids?"

She frowned at him. "You underestimate those little fellas. I saw them run a little while ago. You better get ready, bud, because they may just leave us in their smoke."

Todd grabbed her around the waist and she grabbed him around the waist again. When his foreman who was overseeing the race said, "Ready, set, go," it was as if chaos broke out. Kids started running and Ginny yanked on his waist; he had a delayed reaction and stumbled and then she stumbled. They managed to stay upright but they were behind already. He was frankly quite embarrassed and then she nudged him— well, she didn't nudge him; she rammed an elbow in his waist. "Come on, Todd. Get with the program."

He laughed and then, taking the initiative, he started running. Basically, he picked her up against his side and he started hopping, running, hopping, running as he watched everybody else. But they didn't make it far. Two little girls fell in front of them and instead of running over them, he tried to dodge them but got off-balance. He and Ginny went down in a pile of laughter and giggles. She landed on top of him and then she rolled over on the ground, and he was looking down at her, completely lost. He watched the boys as they ran across the finish line and then turned and started jumping up and down and then started coming back their way. He looked down into her laughing face. The face he was really tempted to kiss. The sensation hit him so hard it was beginning to be ridiculous how much he was thinking about kissing her again. She was beautiful, she was funny, fun to be around, and smart. He was quickly realizing there was so much about Ginny that appealed to him that he wasn't sure what in the world he was going to do. Right now, he grinned at her. "Well, you're right—we lost, and here they come to gloat. You called it."

"I did, but I kind of felt like they would. This isn't easy, this running with three legs. Especially when I'm shorter than you. Those two—they're pretty matched up…fairly decent heights and speeds. So don't feel too bad, Todd."

The kids arrived and circled them. All of them

were jumping up and down, yelling and laughing. The two boys were untying their legs; they looked really proud of themselves.

"We told you we'd beat you." Bo nudged his partner, who grinned like a hyena.

"Yeah, we did, and now we get the prize."

"What is the prize?" Todd asked, realizing that he didn't even know what they lost, hoping it was something good.

He helped Ginny up. She came to a sitting position and grinned at the kids. "It's that big—well, you get two of them. There are water guns over there. They've got y'alls names on them now. Well, not really your names but you know what I mean—that's what you win."

The boys yelled with delight and raced across to the table where some pretty high-powered water guns awaited. Just exactly what two little boys like that would want. If they could find water right now, they figured that everybody in the place was fixing to get soaked down.

He stared at her after everybody went to inspect

the water guns. "Did you pick those out? They look pretty fun."

"I did. I had them pick them up the other day when they went into town for me. I had a feeling that if there were some older kids here, girls or boys, then that's who would win, so I figured either one—girl or boy—would enjoy those. I used to love to shoot water pistols. 'Course, now I have Loretta and I find target practice with her is really fun. Give me a bunch of aluminum cans and I can have at it."

He laughed. "Well, right now I'm glad about that because you just remember to keep your Loretta with you when you're out in that buggy all by yourself."

"I will. I don't have it with me today because of this but when all the kiddos and all the people are gone tomorrow, I'll stash her on that rack under my seat."

"Sounds perfect. I might, matter of fact, have a holster that fits on that right there by the steering wheel—easier access. I think I'll have them attach that for you and then you'll have it closer to you—won't have to reach up under anything to get it, just grab it from right there."

He was untying the rope around their ankles.

"Well, thanks, Todd. I'm really not thinking I'm going to run into your mountain lion but just in case, I appreciate your concern."

He stared at her, still wanting to kiss her. He couldn't help it; he put his arm around her and tugged her into his side. Her big ole eyes looked up at him and he wondered whether she was thinking about kissing him too. "Ginny, I'm serious. I don't really want anything happening to you and I don't want you taking any chances, okay?"

She placed her hand on his heart. "I'll be careful. I'm kind of fond of you too. So, you take care of yourself too, okay?"

He smiled and, unable to help himself, he bent down and gave her a quick kiss on the lips.

Ginny walked over to the jelly table after Todd had gone back to help with the wine stomping. Allie was watching her with a smug look on her face. Ginny knew before she said anything what she had watched.

"That was sweet." Allie sounded like the Cheshire cat from Alice in Wonderland.

Ginny felt a little bit like Alice at the moment, as if she had fallen through the rabbit's hole and was in a whole different world than what she was used to.

"Yeah, about that…I might be in trouble."

"I think that's wonderful. I'm glad you're at least kind of exploring it and giving it a shot."

"It's almost like I don't have any choice. When he pulls me close and looks at me like that, it's like something inside me just gives up. It's the strangest feeling. I mean, seriously, Allie, I'm about as kick-butt as it comes: independent, straight shooter, too strong-willed to feel like anybody could put up with me for very long. And yet, like I say, when he looks at me lately, I don't even fight—I just say yes. And that worries me."

Allie looked at the old woman at the end of the table. "Clara, I'm going to take a break. Y'all think you can handle it now that the race is over?"

Clara grinned at her and Ethel did too. "Oh, we can handle this. You two go talk. And don't think we didn't see our fellow giving you a little peck on the lips there. And we like it, don't we, Ethel?"

Ethel was beaming. "Yes, we do. That boy works way too hard and he goes home to that empty house. Ever since you've been here, you two seemed a little bit stiff, like when you came up there the other day to look at the jelly, and we were kind of worried. Yup, y'all didn't act like newlyweds. And, to be honest, we heard a rumor that y'all might have a fake marriage. That there was something in his granddaddy's will that made him have to get married. And we were worried. But I ain't never seen Todd McCoy look at somebody so gentle-like and so full of longing. So, yeah, you go on back over there and you hang close to that man because we like what we're seeing."

Ginny just stared at the two ladies, taken aback at what they were saying. But she felt glad that they approved. And wondered how in the world they had heard the rumor.

Allie got up and grinned at her. "See? They know a good thing when they see it. I think you two are adorable together. And I'm really happy to have you as a sister-in-law."

The ladies grinned and winked and waved at them and then they headed out. Ginny was relieved to get away. Things were happening too fast; she felt so out of her comfort zone. She did not like being out of her comfort zone. She was used to being in control; she was used to being the one who drove things, directed the way things were going to go. She felt as if she were being pulled and swept away on somebody else's agenda. But it wasn't as if she wanted to get off the merry-go-round. And that was the weird part—she liked it too much.

CHAPTER TWENTY

Morgan arrived while the grape stomping was going on. When Allie and Ginny joined Wade and Morgan and Todd to watch, it was the first time Ginny had been around Todd's brother. He was gorgeous. He was a couple of years older and had a very strong resemblance to the brothers but he was a more refined look and she could see him in the position that he was in, traveling the world and dealing with hotel enterprises and different things that their hotel chain dealt with. Although she could see him on a horse, too. It was funny how the clothes changed a man's look. Getting off the plane, he was still in dress slacks, expensive Italian-looking shoes, and dress shirt. She assumed he either had a suit jacket or sports coat somewhere near; he looked relaxed, elegant, and gorgeous. And completely not her type. But she had a feeling that if the man changed into jeans and boots and threw a cowboy hat on his head, he would look right at home too.

Ginny took in all three of the men together; they were a gorgeous lot. Tall, dark, and handsome, with strong jaws. Todd had a curliness to his hair that the other men didn't have. And though Wade and Morgan were both amazingly handsome men, they did nothing for her in the butterfly department. But all she had to do was look at Todd McCoy and her heart started thumping, butterflies started going crazy, and her knees got weak. Thankfully, it didn't happen all at once and make her a total weakling, having to sit down. But goodness gracious, the man *did* have an effect on her. And when he smiled like he was doing right now—oh lordy, she was a goner.

"Morgan, this is Ginny. I'm glad you came down

and got to meet her. She is a lot of the reason this festival is the success it is today. With both my head overseer and wine master leaving, I was kind of in a predicament. She jumped right in there and has done pretty well."

Morgan held his hand out and smiled at her. But there was a contemplative look in his eyes as she put her hand in his. "Nice to meet you, Ginny. We're very lucky that you and Todd could come to an agreement and both of you could benefit from this craziness that our granddad has done with his will." He had let go of her hand and she had placed hers on her hips and nodded.

"I am too. I'd been having to scramble if it hadn't been for Allie here and Wade realizing that I could get in here and Todd and I would benefit each other."

Todd put his arm over her shoulders and it seemed as if it were quite comfortable for him to do. And she didn't mind at all. But there was that unsettling feeling inside her that they were getting very chummy together and in three weeks, things would end. Like they should. Because she was kind of living in a fairy-tale world at the moment. She didn't do fairy tales too well.

"Yeah, Allie and I were very glad to be able to connect you two on this." Wade smiled.

She really liked Wade. Allie had gotten a good fella. And Ginny had really given him a hard time when he had proposed his crazy scheme to her best friend.

"I have to say, your granddaddy must have been one-of-a-kind because he really came up with a weird idea but it saved mine and Allie's bacon. I'm looking forward to getting back to my vineyard and working the ground again. But like I told Todd here, I love y'alls vineyard. It's something to be very proud of. I'm going to go spend time in the blending room tomorrow and I can't wait. I'm hoping that maybe Todd and I can come up with some kind of agreement, if he's got any kind of extra grapes available next year or this year that I could blend with some of mine. Anyway, I'm looking forward to it. I love doing that."

"I think that sounds great. We'll go first thing in the morning." Todd looked at her and grinned. Todd grinned a lot, it seemed, lately. She kept thinking that he didn't grin very much when they first met. She liked the fact that maybe she was helping him loosen up a little bit.

Morgan considered what she was saying, his face thoughtful. "I'll tell you, Todd was telling me about your vineyard and it sounds like you've done a really good job with it. He says your wine is really wonderful. And you know, we're using our wines in the hotels. We have the benefit of having our exclusive hotel lines that can cater to a demographic of people who enjoy wine and they like the McCoy Stonewall wine label. How are you on stock? We could give it a try in some of our places—we could maybe work out a contract, if you've got any available."

Ginny stared at Morgan, her heart paused in disbelief. Now she really did feel as though she needed to sit down. All this time that she had been here, she hadn't even considered the power behind McCoy Stonewall Enterprises and their hotel chain. She swallowed the lump in her throat and blinked hard. She needed to keep it together; she was no emotional pansy. But this was a make-it-or-break-it moment. This could be the biggest break her winery had ever gotten.

"I have a good amount of cases. We have several years' worth. We don't always sell everything but I can promise you they're all really good. Being a boutique winery like we are, we've managed to produce fairly well in the small property that we have. I'm not sure how many cases you're talking about but I would love—I mean, not to get all emotional or anything or overexcited—but I would love to talk with you very seriously about taking on Rossi Rose of Tyler Vineyard's wine." She held her hand out.

Morgan grinned; he grasped it immediately. "I think this could be beneficial for both of us. And we're very grateful for what you've done to help us hang on to our vineyard. That was one reason I came here today. Todd and I had discussed this a couple of days ago. I did some numbers and tested your wine that he sent me with some people who have a really good palate and I think that we could help put Rossi Rose of Tyler Vineyards on the map in a bigger way."

She looked at Todd. "So, you knew about this and didn't tell me?"

"Nope. I just thought, coming from Morgan, that it would mean more. My brother has done amazing things with our hotel chain; he has taken it to levels that we never dreamed. There's a demographic that my granddaddy, in the early days, didn't even have on his map. We have different levels of our hotels that cater to different levels of pocketbooks—those for families and those for business and those for exclusive resorts—and that's where your wine will be served. And like you were saying with our grapes, if you're as good at blending as you say you are, then you come up with something that we can bring in together and contract out some grapes to you so that you can enlarge, then we're on board."

Ginny was more than overwhelmed. And she must have looked it because Allie reached out, put a hand on her arm, and squeezed.

"Ginny, don't think that this isn't because of your hard work. They wouldn't be offering you this if it wasn't that you're really good at what you do. And I'm just really thrilled for you."

Ginny nodded at her friend and tried to smile but

she was so overwhelmed that it was hard even to do that without grinning like an idiot. She looked from Todd to Wade, who was smiling, to Morgan, who was quiet but had a very serious expression on his face. The man was all business. She loved him dearly.

She walked over and threw her arms around his neck and gave him a big hug. "Morgan McCoy, I just want to give you a hug and I can tell you I'm not a hugger." She laughed and stepped back from him. The smile she had been trying to form burst through her face and then she spun and threw herself into Todd's waiting arms. "Thank you, Todd, thank you for believing in me." She leaned back and looked at him; he was grinning. "From where we started, you really didn't take me seriously, and I have to say that really kind of made me mad. But honestly, you didn't have to do this. I'm not turning it down because it's everything I ever dreamed of. I just needed a shot to get myself out there."

He held her tight and his eyes bore into hers. "When we first met, I was a dang fool. I was closed up and not listening. But I'm listening now and like

Morgan said, this is going to be good for both of us."

She turned, still in his arms, and smiled at everybody. "I think we should celebrate, if we could find some champagne somewhere. I don't drink much but I would sure celebrate this with a glass of champagne."

Wade grinned. Todd did, too, and Morgan crossed his arms and laughed. "I'd say we can go find some of that. And I agree this needs to be celebrated, I'm not happy about Granddaddy's will but I'm very pleased that Wade and Todd were able to find people to help them. I'm excited that Wade and Allie fell in love in the process—totally shocked. The odds were against them but it's really cool to see and I know Granddaddy would be happy about that. And you two look very chummy. I know y'all have a business deal going and I'm not going to assume anything other than the fact that y'all work well together. So even if you part ways at the end of the three months, this has been a good experience for Todd and our winery and yours too. I think when we have that glass of champagne; we'll have to toast Granddaddy too. As crazy as his idea was, it's been a success so far."

He looked at Wade and Allie. "And he might even get some great-grandkids from these two. I know he'd be smiling down from heaven about that. I have to admit, it would be really cool to see some kids running around these fields like we used to."

Ginny didn't know what to say to what Todd's brother had just said. She had no idea where they were headed and she wasn't going to say because, personally, she was so unsure of everything. But what Morgan said was true; this had been an amazing experience and no matter what happened to them personally at the end of this, with what she had just been offered, and even before that, just getting her vineyard safely in her name and setting her mom and dad up for retirement, was a win for her. This new deal was just an extraordinary win-win for the future.

If she had this deal with Todd's winery, then it would help relieve some stress off her shoulders for future harvests. That was something she had never really had. Her vineyard was built on small orders, not large orders. It was amazing. She smiled at Todd; he was still holding her. And then she kissed him on the cheek. "Thank you." Then she stepped back and put a little distance between them. "Well, either we go find that champagne or I think we roll up our pant legs and squash some grapes."

The next day, Todd met Ginny at the back barns where they were going to go to the blending room. He had thought about her all night. Who was he kidding—he thought about her all day these days. He and Morgan had talked late into the night after Wade and Allie had gone back to the ranch. Morgan had asked him whether he was falling in love with Ginny. He told his brother he thought he might be but that it was complicated. Everything about Ginny was complicated. Just because he was falling in love with her didn't mean that she would stay. Not when her heart and soul was in Tyler, Texas with Rossi Rose of Tyler Vineyards.

Morgan had clamped him on the shoulder and squeezed hard before he went up for the night and told him he had his blessing and that from what he saw, they were a really perfect match, and he was pleased for Todd. After Morgan had gone up, Todd had sat there on the porch, taking in everything that had happened, taking in his future and thinking about what a life with Ginny would be like. His answer was easy: it would be a firecracker existence; there would be happy times and there would be fiery times. They would have disagreements and then they would make up. The thought had him grinning. One thing about Ginny Rossi McCoy—there would never be a boring moment and he liked that. She was everything he never knew he needed or wanted. And yet, here she was, and all he had to do was figure out how to get her to stay.

And as he saw her driving up in the ATV with that pink shotgun sticking out of the holster that he had snapped on to the bar near the steering wheel, he smiled. He got a vision of her riding around every day, looking like that, looking like the queen of this vineyard. But she was the queen of the Rossi Rose of Tyler Vineyards and that was a five- to six-hour drive from them—less than an hour flight—but he didn't want to leave his vineyard and live in Tyler. And he had the sinking feeling, looking at her, that as much as she seemed to enjoy his vineyard, she wouldn't want to give it up and live here. He was in a dilemma.

"Morning, sunshine," he said as she jumped from the ATV and strode toward him. He reached for her as she made it to him and embraced her. Getting comfortable doing that now. He gave her a gentle kiss on the lips and she accepted it. Her eyes searched his, sparking with excitement.

"Good morning to you, cowboy. Let's get in there. Today is the day we're going to have fun, fun, fun."

He laughed hard. And then, arm in arm, they strode into the barn and headed toward the blending room.

By the time they had finished in the blending room, it was getting late. She had had so much fun and Todd had, too. She had blended a major variation of grape blends and added blends from different types of oak barrels, giving them each different types of flavors.

She was amazed from what she had to choose from: they had oak barrels from Italy and different locations. It seemed they had every type of barrel there was. Each barrel gave the wine grapes that were in it a different blend, a different dimension.

It was the most fun she had ever had when it came to her vineyards. In truth, the best time she'd ever had—all of her best times since Kyle's death—had been spent with her vineyards. And as she slid into the seat of her ATV, she sighed, watching as the sun started to set in the distance. She knew that they were on the right track for something amazing.

And she thought Todd was in agreement. He had genuinely seemed thrilled with watching her and he had enjoyed tasting things that she came up with. And they were going to try some blends for next year. It was thrilling.

He stared at her. "Ginny, I honestly would offer you the job of master winemaker here. I don't think we've ever had such enthusiasm in the blending room. It was thrilling to watch. And I can't wait for some of the blends to mature."

Her heart thundered as she looked at him. Master winemaker of this vineyard was not something she had thought about being offered. "Are you serious?"

"I'm dead serious. I know you're going back to Tyler—I know that's where your heart is—but if something were to happen and your mom and dad didn't come through on this deal for you, honey, you've got a job here."

Staring at him, she suddenly fought back tears. She had a *job* here. He wasn't offering her the position as his wife here but as master winemaker. Suddenly, that knowledge hurt deeply. She fought for control. *This was silly—why was she thinking like that?* "Thank you, Todd. I would consider it—it's amazing, really. But I'm going back to Tyler. My mom and dad are going to take the money—I'm going to talk to them about it tomorrow. What we agreed with beforehand is going to pay them off and give them an extremely comfortable retirement. And they're going to let me take over the winery, in my name. And with this new deal that we're working out with the hotels, I'll be able to give them a yearly dividend, so that'll even add to the deal for them. So I guess we're all set that at the end of our time, we've got a plan. Anyway, I'm tired. I'm going to head back to the house and I'll be back here tomorrow. I guess I'll see you back at the house?"

He had a strange look on his face but she tried not to think about that. He looked almost…sad? Stunned? She wasn't sure why. He was the one who offered her the master winemaker position. He was the one who had opened up the conversation about the end of her time here and the fact that it wouldn't end with her being his wife.

"Yeah, I'll be up in a few minutes. I need to close up for the night. I'll follow you in the truck in a bit. You sleep good. And I know we had lunch here and snacked on cheese and crackers all day, but I'm sure there's food in the fridge for you if you want something to eat."

"Yeah, I'm sure. See you later." She cranked the key on the ATV, put it in gear and he stepped out of the way. She stepped on the gas pedal; the ATV shot forward and in a wide arc, she turned it around, headed back through the vineyards toward the house. As she drove, she wasn't even aware for a minute that tears were rolling down her cheeks. The wind chilled them and she wiped them away with the back of her hand. The sun was setting behind her. Dusk was falling; shadows filled the gravel drive between the rows of vines. She drove, speeding faster than she should be on the gravel. She realized, looking behind her, that Todd wasn't coming yet.

Knowing that she didn't want to reach the house with tears on her face if Mavis was there—she didn't want her to see her cry—Ginny pulled over in the shadows and let the tears fall. Wade and Allie had made a life of it. They were happy. They were going to have children. They were going to have a future together. They had made it—yeah, the odds had been against them but they had made it. And she had never even thought about anything past the agreement. She hadn't thought about any of that.

Until now, she never realized how badly she wanted it. How bad it would hurt when she had to say good-bye. She told herself it wouldn't work, anyway:

her heart was in Tyler. How could they make it work when she wanted to be in Tyler and he wanted to be here, even if they did have a jet that could get them back and forth in no time at all? And why was she even thinking about coming up with a compromise? She would live here and fly out to her vineyard whenever possible—or at least once a week or twice a month or a week out of the month. The possibilities were there; it could be worked out. They had a plane, for crying out loud. Well, she didn't have a plane; Todd had a plane.

They had the means; he never really put off an air—it was easy to forget that Todd McCoy and his brothers were billionaires. They were so down-to-earth, it was so hard to believe. But being billionaires, they had assets that enabled a life that she had never thought about until now. So the logistics of her beloved vineyard in Tyler and his beloved vineyard here—it could probably be worked out. But he hadn't offered that.

She sniffed, wiped her eyes, and took a deep

breath. Then she had the funniest feeling that she was being watched. In the now dwindling light, she glanced around, down the vineyard lane to her left and then down the vineyard lane to her right. She froze. There, sitting about a hundred feet from her, was a mountain lion. Its eyes caught the faint light and she saw, in the shadows, its tail swish. Her heart thundered as she slowly reached for Loretta.

CHAPTER TWENTY-ONE

Todd didn't go back in the winery; he didn't go anywhere except to the truck, where he propped his elbows on the edge of the truck bed and looked out across the vineyard, watching the taillights of the ATV disappear into the shadowy night, over the hill and out of view. He saw the look in Ginny's eyes when he had offered her the master winemaker position. There had been disappointment there but she had made it clear that her parents were going to take the deal and she was going back to Tyler. It had taken everything in him to not ask her to stay with him. He wanted to but he didn't want to compromise her, didn't want her to think she—who was he kidding? He didn't want her to tell him no. He didn't want to risk asking her to stay to be his wife, live on his property, and have babies with him and have a future here. He didn't want to ask her to put her dream on hold and come make a new dream with him. He didn't want to risk rejection.

He was a fool. He still had time. But she had plans and all her plans—despite the kisses and the hugs and the friendship they had held—all her plans were still back in Tyler. All her plans were still business. Yeah, business with some benefits, with some great kisses—that was all it was. And he was a coward. He raked his hand through his hair. He loved her. He did, but he wasn't going to ask her to do that. Even though logistically speaking, they did have the means to get back and forth.

But she had all of her past and all of her future wrapped up in being on that vineyard and his vineyard was too big; he needed to be here. But it hit him—he could live in Tyler. He could live in Tyler and he could fly here every day if he had to. Heck, people did that—

people commuted every day on a plane for business trips. Why couldn't he do that? He never wanted to be in a plane all the time like Morgan was practically, but for Ginny he would. He straightened and reached for the truck door. He had to get to her.

Just as he yanked the door open, he heard Loretta fire twice. He threw himself into the truck, cranked the engine, and tore out of there, driving down the gravel track, *she had not fired that gun without a reason.* All he could think was the mountain lion was back. *The mountain lion was here.* Everything that they thought wouldn't happen was happening. His gut told him so, but he prayed it was wrong as he searched ahead of him. He was traveling fast; he hit one of the hills and the truck flew into the air. It came down hard and everything in the truck bounced as it landed. He straightened out, keeping it on the road, keeping it going over the next hill.

He spotted her vehicle. The lights were shining, parked in the vineyard against the grapevines. He reached behind him for the rifle that he had started carrying on the rifle hook of his back windshield. He threw the truck into park and opened the door, putting a round in the chamber as he got out.

"Ginny," he called. He didn't hear anything as he ran forward toward the ATV. "Ginny, answer me." Nothing. He looked left and he looked right. He walked forward into the lane, looking down the rows and listening for any sound. He went back to the ATV. He bent down and looked at where her feet were. He saw the shells. She was heading left. He saw the paw print and then the other. He yelled, "Ginny, for crying out loud, answer me!"

He ran forward, trying to follow her footprints. But it was too dark and he lost sight of them. Then he heard her.

"I'm here, Todd."

He spun around and she stood there, Loretta pointed down and hanging at her side.

"He's gone."

He ran forward and pulled her into his arms. "Are you okay?" She buried her face in his shoulder and nodded. He felt her shake. His Ginny, who was so strong and brave and bold, trembled. He held the gun pointed down and held her as tightly as he could with one arm. He knew Loretta was pointed down and out of bullets, so he didn't have to worry about that; she had shot twice, so there was nothing left in it unless she had managed to reload. "You're not going to shoot me with that thing, are you?"

She laughed softly against his shoulder. "No. It seems that when I'm scared, I can't shoot the broad side of a barn. The cat got away."

"I don't care what he did as long as he didn't hurt you."

"You probably need to warn somebody."

"I will. You just stand still—let me hold you while I make the phone call." He pulled the phone out of his pocket, hit the speed dial and called Wade. "We spotted the cat again. It tried to attack Ginny. I've got her here—she's fine. She's shaken up. Can you make the calls to get somebody out here? Warn people. We're in the fields before you get to the wine vat."

"I've got it. We'll be there soon. You take care of her."

He hung up. He looked in the distance and saw truck lights coming. He realized it was probably Morgan. If Morgan had been out—he had been the only one around this late at night—then he would've been coming to see what was going on. Gunshots on the vineyard weren't normal.

He kissed her forehead. "Ginny," he said. "All I could think of when I heard that gun go off was that I lost you."

She looked at him. "Todd, when I saw that cat and he charged me and I pulled that trigger and missed, all I could think about was that I was about to die and that I hadn't told you that I loved you."

He grinned like a fool, like the fool for her that he was. "Ginny Rossi McCoy, I love you. And I don't care what we have to do but I want you to be my wife from this day forward and every day after that. I want you in my life. And if I have to fly from Tyler every day to come to this vineyard, then that's what I'll do. But I'm telling you right here and now, it's going to take a lot for you to get rid of me."

Her smile dazzled him. "Todd McCoy, you just try to get rid of me. 'Cuz I can tell you right now, I'm one stubborn woman and it's going to be really hard for you to run me off."

He laughed and then he kissed her, keeping one eye open, looking for a cat. But he knew Morgan was coming and everything was going to be okay.

EPILOGUE

It was a gorgeous night in Texas with the stars shining brightly as the band played country music love songs as everyone danced. Ginny had never in her life felt so content and happy. Really happy as her love held her in his arms and whispered his love in her ear as they danced a fast two-step around the dance floor.

"I'm in love with you, Mrs. McCoy," Todd whispered, his warm breath tickling her ear and sending lovely tingles of happiness down her spine. He spun her out from him, his fingers holding hers lightly as she twirled and spun back into his waiting arms and warm embrace she craved.

"And I love you more," she said, kissing his smiling lips, loving that she could do that and have no regrets. He was all hers and she was his and they shared a passion in love, in business and friendship. How it had happened still mystified both of them but it had happened—thank goodness. And from the most unlikely of circumstances. "If your granddaddy materialized right now I'd give him a huge hug and kiss on both cheeks for forcing us into this marriage."

"He would love you. Here's an idea kiss me instead." Todd grinned wickedly and she laughed, then did as he asked as the song ended and the crowd clapped, they pulled away from the kiss and laughed together as they looked about the circle of friends and family who had come to their wedding reception.

Penny, Todd's grandfather's friend, who knew all about the will and peculiar marriage demands came toward them. She had thrown this party for them, just as she'd thrown one for Wade and Allie. Granddaddy's brother, Talbert, came with Penny. Talbert was the grandfather of Caroline, Denton, Ash, and Beck, all of

Todd's cousins. She hadn't met all of them yet but she loved Talbert and Caroline.

"You two look mighty happy," Talbert said, grinning big. He was a Texas oil tycoon but looked as down to earth as a cowboy could get in his jeans with his western cut suede jacket and Cowboy hat. "Your granddaddy is probably dancing a jig up in heaven over what that crazy will of his has produced."

Ginny was startled by the statement and a quick look at Todd said he was too.

"You knew, Uncle Talbert?" Todd asked.

The older man's eyes crinkled at the edges. "Yes, mind you though, none of my grandkids know it. Just me, Penny and Cal. Unless he told someone I don't know about we're it I think. Who knows, there could be more. J.D. was always full of surprises. And this is one that I'm as tickled about as a newborn calf chasing a butterfly." He grinned roguishly. "Might even surprise my bunch with some similar stipulations if one of them doesn't get me some great-grandkids soon. And I'm not joking."

"Really," Ginny said, thinking of Caroline and

how much she would hate such a thing. "Might be safer for you to wait till you pass on. I'm not sure I'd want to tangle with Caroline if she were forced to get married. Of course, we all hope you hang around for a very long time." She gave him an affectionate hug.

"I plan on it, that's why I'd have to come up with a bit of a different plan."

Todd frowned. "I second what Ginny said. You want to make the cousins mad then toss this at them. I wasn't happy one bit and Morgan is like a bull in a rodeo chute. He's so knotted up over it I don't know if he'll ever forgive granddaddy."

Penny sighed. "I hope he gets over that. I hope he doesn't do anything foolish and not comply with the will's stipulations when he hears them on Monday."

Todd pulled Ginny into his side and she went willingly. "I've told him he might get as lucky at me and Wade, but he's not happy still. You know him, he and granddaddy clashed hard, they were so much alike. Hard–headed, the both of them." He kissed Ginny's forehead. "But Morgan's no fool. He's worked too hard for the McCoy Stonewall Hotel and Resort

Division to walk away without a fight. Granddaddy knew it. So, we'll just have to hope it all works out."

Talbert grinned. "It'll sure be fun to see that calm, cool, collected cowboy turned city slicker take up the challenge. I told J.D. he was crazy but now I think he was a genius."

Ginny smiled and wrapped her arms tightly around Todd and looked up into his eyes. "I think he was brilliant."

Todd kissed the tip of her nose. "I'm glad his crazy fiasco of a will brought us together...but I'm still not certain everyone forced to get married would be so lucky."

Penny sighed. "I love y'all's happy ending."

"Me too," Ginny said as Caroline walked up.

"What are you four conspiring about over here," Caroline asked looking around the group. She was dazzling in a slinky silver dress that set off her brunette hair. She and Ginny had become fast friends and were very similar in personalities, just like Allie had told her they were.

Ginny grinned. "We're talking about how smart

Todd's granddaddy was in coming up with this will of his. I think you need to have to do it too."

Everyone chuckled, and Talbert grinned like a sneaky kid about to play a trick.

Caroline scoffed, "Oh no, not me. Can you imagine some poor fella having to marry me for some reason other than love? It's going to be hard enough for someone who happens to have the misfortune to fall in love with me. I'm pretty set in my ways."

Morgan walked up with Wade and Allie.

"You can say that again," he said, smiling at his cousin.

Everyone was grinning at the two of them.

Caroline shot him a warning. "I was just saying if I was forced to do what you and your brothers have been forced to do, it would not be pretty. I'm not going to lie, it would probably be impossible for me to find someone to go along with the plan. I feel for you Morgan, since it's your turn next." She looked at her granddaddy. "Don't be getting any ideas, Granddad."

Talbert hitched a brow and chuckled and Ginny wondered what the old man would do in the end?

Morgan frowned. "We'll see what the will has in store for me, but Granddaddy knew I'm not good at being controlled."

"You aren't good at loosing either," Wade pointed out.

Todd agreed, "No, you're not. So just get ready, brother, you're going to do it."

"We'll see." Morgan's expression was hard.

Ginny couldn't help hoping that the miracles hadn't stopped and that somewhere out there was the perfect match for her brother-in-law. Of all the brothers, he seemed the most untouchable. His granddaddy probably wanted to change that.

It would be interesting to see what happened. She met Allie's bright eyes and winked. Her friend's eyes sparkled. They were true believers in J.D.'s plan.

She'd found the love of her life and couldn't imagine life without Todd.

She looked up at him as the music began to play. "I think they're playing a song that's calling our names."

"Well, then let's get back out there. Any excuse to

hold you in my arms is good for me."

And as everyone watched, he swept her onto the dance floor. "You make me happy, Ginny. I love you."

"I love you more," she laughed.

"We'll have to debate that later when we're alone," he whispered and snuggled her closer.

"I was hoping you'd say that," she sighed contently and nestled her cheek against his heart. She was right where she was supposed to be.

Thanks, J.D., I love you too.

Check out the next book in the McCoy Billionaire Brothers series, HER BILLIONAIRE COWBOY'S TROUBLE IN PARADISE

About the Author

Hope Moore is the pen name of an award-winning author who lives deep in the heart of Texas surrounded by Christian cowboys who give her inspiration for all of her inspirational sweet romances. She loves writing clean & wholesome, swoon worthy romances for all of her fans to enjoy and share with everyone. Her heartwarming, feel good romances are full of humor and heart, and gorgeous cowboys and heroes to love. And the spunky women they fall in love with and live happily-ever-after.

When she isn't writing, she's trying very hard not to cook, since she could live on peanut butter sandwiches, shredded wheat, coffee...and cheesecake why should she cook? She loves writing though and creating new stories is her passion. Though she does love shoes, she's admitted she has an addiction and tries really hard to stay out of shoe stores. She, however, is not addicted to social media and chooses to write instead of surf FB - but she LOVES her readers so she's working on a free novella just for you and if you sign up for her newsletter she will send it to you as soon as its ready! You'll also receive snippets of her adventures, along with special deals, sneak peaks of soon-to-be released books and of course any sales she might be having.

She promises she will not spam you, she hates to be spammed also, so she wouldn't dare do that to people she's crazy about (that means YOU). You can unsubscribe at any time.

Sign up for my newsletter:
www.subscribepage.com/hopemooresignup

I can't wait to hear from you.

Hope Moore~
Always hoping for more love, laughter and reading for you every day of your life!

Made in the USA
Columbia, SC
17 November 2020

24793008R00134